MY
WIFE
BECOMES
A
FIELD

New writing

First Published by
The Ludovic Press
2007

ISBN 978-0-9553716-1-5

MY
WIFE
BECOMES
A
FIELD

LUDOVIC PRESS
THIRD FLOOR
65 GLASSFORD STREET
GLASGOW
G1 1UB

www.johnstonewritersgroup.com

MY
WIFE
BECOMES
A
FIELD

EDITED BY

IAN HUNTER
AND
WILLIAM PURCELL
AND
MAUREEN BLAKE

INTRODUCTION

It's a strange paradox that all fiction is fantastic, made-up, make-believe, lies. Even when it is as fantastical as Brian Hannan's "Snailbait" or Fiona Lindsay's wonderfully naturalistic "Nothing Special". Yet at its best fiction is there to reveal some truth, to connect with the reader, either by being explicit or igniting a spark, a light in the heart or mind of those who let the words before them pass through their heads.

My Wife Becomes a Field is full of such lies and deceits, and truths. Whether it is a truth borne of experience, or hope, or dreams dashed. Of birth, renewal, or endings. It is the work of the writer to bear witness, to themselves and the world around them, particularly in the form of poetry, where every word counts.

All of the poets collected here know how to use words to make a point, to leave an after taste. Here you have Jim Carruth, acknowledged as an important rural voice, trading poetry blows with old hands such as Betty McKellar and Jack Hastie. Although it is a poetry bout bound to go the distance as they all drink from the same natural spring. Bobby Lauder, on the other hand, plucks his poetic gems from newspaper headlines, while G.I Campbell merely has to open the flood gates and release the dark waters that pour from his teenage worldview. George Colkitto, a new poet, demonstrates that he is already a good one, knowing which words to use and how to place them so that the sum is greater than the parts

But don't be fooled into thinking that Field is just about poetry.

It is also the laconic observations of Clive Briggs, the authentic military voice of John Coughlan, the emergence of a major talent in Caro Ramsay, the historical verve of Lilias

Michael which creates a fusion of fact and fiction, the eerie entertainment of Eleanor Jeffrey; and more, so much more.

Truths, and lies, and everything in between.

Ian Hunter
Winter 2006

Brian Hannan

Snailbait

A gang of polar bears unloaded a dragon from a three-masted schooner under the shadow of the water clock. High above the harbour, the glass pillars of the Fantastiquarium sparkled in the early morning sunshine. Baimbo, eating a bowl of thin porridge at the kitchen window, knew how the creature felt. He was all trussed up in his school uniform, dreading the first day of high school.

'Don't sit anywhere beside me in the exam, slug face,' said Vebeonrea, his twin sister, undoing the scarf on her head and patting the long ponytail into place.

Anyone could see they were not identical. He had thick black curly hair and dark skin. She was blonde and fair. He had brown eyes and a kind of squashed face. She had green tiptoe eyes and a perky nose and a little mole on her chin that looked like a drip of honey.

Baimbo clattered his empty bowl on the table. 'I'll sit anywhere I want.'

Vebeonrea yelled, 'Uncle Ransalbane, he's not made his bed.'

Baimbo glanced anxiously at the black wooden door. The kitchen smelled of boiled cabbage and roasted sweat. Baimbo slept on the floor among splinters as sharp as nails. Cracked bricks shiny with damp held up the sloping attic roof. The room was big enough for a small stove, sink, tiny rickety table and a chair. The door opened and his uncle charged in and tripped over the grey blankets on the floor. Ransalbane growled himself upright. He wore a dark green tweed coat dangling loose on his skinny body and faded brown leather sandals with the flaps undone. He smelled as if he had taken a bath in dust.

'Widosporous,' shouted Ransalbane, clutching his thick black beard with both hands.

Baimbo never heard anyone else in Bal Tyre say this word. He didn't know what it meant, except that his uncle was angry once again.

Vebeonrea stroked the tip of her ponytail and gave a loud sigh, 'He's got porridge on his new tie.'

Baimbo knew without looking that she would be right. How could he have been so clumsy, especially today.

' Branka, ' growled his uncle.

That was another angry word. Baimbo backed into the broken edges of brick while Vebeonrea dusted down her dark blue skirt and gave him a little smile and walked into the hallway. She removed her bead-trimmed pink fonica coat from the wooden peg and let down the hood very gently over her ponytail. On her shoulder she swung a new straw bag decorated with dried pilden leaves that somehow she had persuaded her impoverished uncle to buy.

'Wish me luck,' she said.

Ransalbane let go of his beard. 'Good luck.'

As her boots clacked down the stairs, Baimbo picked up the blankets. Ransalbane turned on Baimbo and rasped, 'You've not even done the lightfish.'

Suddenly his uncle ran out of words and stood with his mouth open, showing the glass fillings on his teeth. No words were worse than even words Baimbo did not understand. Baimbo was not prepared for what happened next. He let out a yelp as he was yanked backwards by the hair and dragged over to the sink. His knee knocked over the chair, the table rattled and with a steady glug-glug a capsized milk bottle emptied its contents onto the floor.

His uncle found his voice. ' You would! Today of all days. Have you any idea how important this day is? Any idea at all? This isn't just about you moping because you can't get out to play. This isn't about you not being able to get up when you're called or leaving everything till the last minute. This is different. This is ....'

Then Baimbo's hair was let go and he felt he was going to be sick. He could hear his uncle sucking in air in one long wheeze and letting it out in little dribbles.

'Come on,' said his uncle in a completely different voice, like a billowing sail that had run out of storm. ' No point getting all worked up over a wee bit of porridge.'

Baimbo turned round and his uncle was smiling. Well, the beard moved sideways and that was always an indication. His uncle licked the end of his sleeve and leaned over to dab away gently at the stain.

'I'll do the dishes and you do the lightfish,' said his uncle in his normal voice. 'How's that?' He gave a practiced chuckle.

3

'But don't think I'm going anywhere near that bed of yours. Never know what dangers lurk there.'

Even with his stinging head, Baimbo thought it sensible to laugh. He was used to his uncle's outbursts. At times like this, when his uncle was smiling, he wanted to keep him happy.

'Don't worry, uncle. I won't be late. I'll do what the teacher tells me. I won't answer back. I'll keep my fists to myself.'

But that wasn't enough for Ransalbane. His uncle added, 'And no peashooter. And stay away from Kimkrill when you go outside. And don't dare come home from school with a black mark.'

Baimbo did not reply, because that would be lying. Instead, he nodded, because that was vague enough to deny later. He rifled among the blankets and picked up the battered schoolbag he had had since low school.

'Wish me luck.'

'Fail the test.'

Baimbo thought he had misheard. 'What?'

'Fail the test.'

Baimbo had never heard anything so ridiculous. Adults told you to work hard and succeed, not fail. Had his uncle gone mad? But Ransalbane had spoken in the slow, patient, manner he used when issuing instructions.

'If I do that, uncle, I won't get to play shotball.'

Ransalbane gave him the long hard stare he used when his instructions were not being obeyed.

'Fail the test.'

Suddenly Baimbo understood. 'Just so's I'm not in the same class as Vebby? You think I'm going to embarrass her, is that it, hurt her chances of getting chosen as a stupid handmaiden for stupid Immelglow? What does she want to do stupid dancing for anyway?'

Ransalbane ignored the outburst and let go of his beard. He picked small hairs from his hands. 'You're better off in the dunces class as far away as possible from any Bassys. Don't go drawing attention to yourself. Not now. Cinter Bassy doesn't know you exist. Let's keep it that way.' He paused, 'I don't want a midnight knock on the door from Mr Thripp.'

Baimbo clattered down the wooden stairs to show he was angry. Vebeonrea had put her uncle up to this. What did she want to become a handmaiden for? There was every chance he would fail anyway. It wasn't as if he was already anywhere near the top of the class. And his uncle refused to help him learn anything. But he desperately wanted to play shotball and the dunce's class didn't get shotball coaching. And why would the Bassys be interested in him? Bassys lived in the palace and were so rich they ate delspelado all day long. The closest he had ever come to a Bassy was seeing a hand waving out of a grand golden coach during the Ghad Mark parade. And Cinter Bassy, who ruled everything, never even left the palace tower.

In the map shop downstairs, the thick dust made him cough. The smell of old parchment was as vivid as a gash. Rolled maps were stacked on shelves on every wall. Baimbo shivered. He hated touching a map. It was like old skin that flaked off in your hand. The only light, more gloom really, came from the high narrow window. Blackfish swimming in glass bowls on the walls gave off crumpled shadows. Worn-down chewed-up charcoal pencils and glass compasses and wooden rulers with obscure markings and the inevitable crusts of burnt bread were scattered on his uncle's wooden desk along with a block of red wax and a wooden seal and a glass jug with a long spout.

He held the jug under the tap of the cask on the floor. He turned the tap and waited till a blackfish the size of his finger and thin as a worm spurted into the jug. He dragged out the ladders from under the desk, climbed to the second top step and tipped up the jug until the fish tumbled into the bowl. Suddenly the glass glowed. When Baimbo had worked his way round the other three glass bowls, the shop was flooded with light.

Outside stank of bear. A bunch of the animals, straight off the nightshift at the glassworks, were playing pork pie first as they waited for the sluice gates to open. But none had a singed bottom. The ticking of the water clock grew louder as the levers of the dam clicked into place.

Baimbo lived in the last house on the quay in a red-brick cottage with a thatched roof. The sea sucked at boats in the harbour. Women with glass buckets stood chattering beside the standpipes along the waterway cut into the black cobblestones. Men in green dungarees sat on squid creels mending nets and polar bears delivered coal to the fish smokery from the back of a steam lorry. Baimbo could smell fish and salt and, boiled cabbage. He sniffed at his new uniform, wondering how the smell had wormed its way into new clothes.

He didn't give a second thought to the dragon chained to an open wagon on the back of the steam engine until he caught sight of the singed white fur bottom at its feet. Kimkrill. Sometimes revenge was all Baimbo thought about. He refused to let anyone take advantage of him. Not even a massive polar bear that had eaten his black-and-white cat. So he had waited till the bear was drunk on heather ale. Drunken bears slept where they fell and one afternoon Baimbo had found Kimkrill slumped near the quayside sluice gate. He daubed sealing wax on its tail and set it on fire. The bear woke up and swiped a chunk out of Baimbo's chin. Now it was Baimbo's turn for revenge. His only weapon was the pea shooter. But the peas had been soaked in vinegar and one in the eye would sting like crazy.

Baimbo crouched down behind a hillock of coiled rope. The dragon strained to lift its long neck but it was held down with metal weights and its mouth was sewn shut with copper wire. Baimbo noticed there were brown whorls on its leathery grey skin and tufts of white hair sprouting from its ears. A deep seeping wound ran under its chin. Baimbo touched the scar under his own chin. The other polar bears were nowhere to be seen. The dragon turned its head and Baimbo found himself staring into its bright green eyes. There was something majestic and hypnotic about the eyes.

Then he heard a deep growl and saw that Kimkrill had spotted him. Baimbo reach for his pea shooter. But the bear simply watched him for a moment with dark cold eyes and bent down and wrenched out one of the dragon's claws.

The dragon's cry was drowned out by a roar as the sluice gates opened and sent an avalanche of water thundering out of the dam and rushing down into an enormous pond. Around the pond showers erupted and the bears danced in the cascading water like children. The water ran along the deep channels and women started filling their buckets. It was called the water clock because time in Bal Tyre was measured by the opening of the sluice gates. The time now was eight o'clock and Baimbo was going to be late.

He saw the green and yellow triple-decker steam bus waiting at the other end of the quayside. He tried to run along the slippery cobbles but his right leg would not let him. The schoolbag was bouncing on his back. He heard the other children shouting as they clambered onto the bus and saw the queue getting smaller and smaller. Then the platform was empty except for the conductress. He felt the sweat run down his face. His foot hurt, the twisted knee throwing his shoulder into a lurching crouch. Faces leered down at him from the top deck windows in between advertisements for the Fantastiquarium. Baimbo realised he was going to miss the bus. If he was late for school, he would fail the test.

Ding-ding!

The bell rang out on the bus and there was a warning whistle of steam as the engine cranked up. He grabbed the metal pole on the platform and swung his bad leg. The boot barely lifted off the ground. He heard an explosion of laughter and saw children heads appear at the top of the stairs craning for a better view. He seized the pole with both hands. His shin cracked against the sharp edge of the platform as his foot again missed the target. The children were hooting and jeering. He was hot with humiliation. The conductress glared at him and rammed her finger on the bell.

Ding-ding !

A girl with the biggest nose he had ever seen appeared on the platform.

'Come on, Snailbait,' said Pig. 'Get your good foot up first.'

Baimbo felt his face go red. She didn't know what she was asking. This was going to get worse. He was holding up the bus now. What if everyone was late and he got into even bigger trouble? He lifted his good leg onto the platform. His body bent over, schoolbag swinging down, face speckled with sweat. He felt the enormous weight of his bad foot as he struggled to raise it. His foot did not want to move.

Ding-ding !

The whole bus was going hysterical. Now everyone would know about him, all these strangers, from the different low schools in Bellsmyre and Silverton and Ridingroad. He wasn't going to be just a boy with a bad limp, he was going to be this stupid wee eejit that couldn't climb onto the school bus.

Ding-ding!

'Close your eyes,' said Pig, softly. Her voice reminded Baimbo of his mother, that calm, that assurance that everything was going to be all right. Tears of frustration ran down his face. But when he opened his eyes, both feet were on the platform.

They sat down on the wooden slatted seats and the bus lurched away along the bumpy cobbles. Pig opened a packet of twisted paper and offered Baimbo a soor ploom. He sucked on the hard green sweet and stared out of the window as he got his breath back.

Away from the quayside, the town sparkled. The houses were tall, two and three storeys high, and built of red sandstone and the roofs were grey slate. Light bounced off tiny pieces of coloured mosaic set into the walls. Brightly painted doors shone with rows and rows of glass beads. Water fancies danced in gardens and small fountains sprayed high arching branches of foam. Every now and then, there was an empty space for a house still missing after the last magic storm. Magic storms used to be rare, several times a year, but in the last month they had been happening once or twice a day. Nobody knew what caused them. Windows and doors and houses would simply disappear. Sometimes people turned into trees or animals or parts of them got larger or smaller. The effect could last for minutes, days or months, or years. Baimbo's foot, for instance, his uncle said, had happened when he was four, although Baimbo could not remember a time when it had not been there. But Pig's nose had grown last year. And a glance around the bus revealed several children with stosie eyes or woggle ears.

'Wish you wouldn't call me Snailbait,' said Baimbo.

'Why not? Everyone else does.'

'They will now you've told them,' he hissed.

'Oh, you thought high school would be a fresh start, is that it?'

'Hadn't thought about it,' he lied. He had been called all sort of names - Lameboy, Hunchback, Crippolina - since leaving the farm at the age of eight and going to low school after he had learned his counting cakes.

'You've got a foot that is just about six times the size of anyone else's foot. I've got a nose that is just about so far out in front of me I have to give it day's notice to blow it. You really think nobody's going to see we are different? You want to make up your own nickname? What would you rather be called? What is it your ugly sister calls you?'

'Slugface.'

'Your stinkster shouldn't be making up horrible nicknames. Family is supposed to be on your side. Anyway, when a friend calls you by a nickname, they say it in a friendly way. Takes the sting out of it. Stops it hurting as much. Then it stops hurting altogether. Then you just about don't notice.'

Baimbo crunched down on the soor ploom. 'What do you think they're going to give us for the test?'

Pig wound a hand in her long red hair. 'History, subterranean geography, illuminated writing, mercantile calculation, indentiquarianism.'

'I wish they'd include shotball.'

'I hate shotball. What's the point of shotball?'

'The one thing my leg is good for is shotball.'

'I don't know why the test has got to last two whole days.'

'You think I'm going to fail?'

She looked round at him, frowning. 'You just about say the strangest things, my little Snailbait. What makes you think you're going to fail?'

Baimbo tried to look unconcerned. 'Nothing. Just something someone said.'

'That Vebeonrea,' snarled Pig. 'She doesn't deserve to be your sister. She's just jealous, my little Snailbait, because one of your feet is bigger than the other.'

The school was attached to the palace. Well, not the palace exactly, but the palace walls, and the back of the palace, not the seafront down by the esplanade and the mosaic square. The school itself was grey sandstone, the first building Baimbo had ever seen without a single piece of decorative glass or mosaic. They came off the bus laughing and shouting but within minutes they were standing in lines in silence as the high black wrought-iron gates clanged shut behind them.

The examination room was like something out of the Fantastiquarium. Long tubes of lightfish were set high into the wood-panelled walls. The fish glowed green and blue and red and gold and when they swam the colours mingled. It was mesmerising and soothing at the same time. At the front was an ordinary blackboard and a desk and chair. Girls were on one side of the classroom and boys on the other. No one sat beside Baimbo. He was used to that, and pleased. One less person close enough to torment him. He just wished he was not sitting in front of Carpacius and Naxmanimede. They had organised the snail race that resulted in his nickname, and spent all low school dreaming up ingenious forms of torture. Their present on his twelfth birthday the week before had been to hold his head underwater.

Carpacius said in his low husky voice, 'We're going to get you at playtime, wastehead.'

Naxmanimede, who had ginger hair and a fat face, drummed his fingers on the desk and chanted, 'Snailbait, Snailbait, Snailbait.'

'We're going to stuff your head down the toilets, bog breath' said Carpacius.

'Snailbait, Snailbait.'

'What are you even bothering sitting the exam for? What's the point of you going to school? Who's ever going to give the likes of you a job? Who needs someone with a boulder for a foot? A glassmaster? Bargemaster?'

'He'd sink the barge. Snailbait, Snailbait.'

'Oh, I know, he wants to be a handmaiden. Want to dance for Immelglow, is that it? You'll need to do something with your hair.' Carpacius leaned over and flipped the ends of Baimbo's hair. ' Never get away with calling that a pony tail.'

Baimbo lunged, knocking over his stool. He was on his feet. 'Shut up. Shut up.'

There was a low growl from the doorway. The class hushed. A polar bear wearing spectacles and a wide-brimmed flowery hat and a blue settle dress closed the door behind her. She padded down the aisle and stood over his desk. She had tiny spots of ink on her nose and smelled of seaweed.

'My name is Miss MacDonald, what's your name?'

'Baimbo, but I was...'

'Another outburst like that, Baimbo, and you will be heading for a black mark.'

Baimbo sat down, fuming. When did polar bears get to become teachers? They usually carried slabs of mosaic, humped sacks of coal, pushed broken-down steam lorries, slouched round the streets getting drunk, or played pork pie first till someone was crippled.

Despite the considerable wobble on her body, Miss MacDonald moved with grace. She walked up to the blackboard and wrote her name out in chalk. Naxmanimede kicked Baimbo under the desk. Miss MacDonald was just explaining that the morning examinations would be history followed by subterranean geography when the door opened.

'You're late.'

Everyone turned round to stare at the blond-haired boy.

'I'm always late,' replied the boy, in a bored voice, as if words were just too much effort.

'Don't be late again.'

'Things don't generally start till I arrive.'

There was a collective intake of breath. Baimbo gave a soft whistle of admiration. Here was someone who could stand up to the teacher. Now see how she liked it.

'Take a seat. You have held up the class long enough.'

'Where am I supposed to sit?' he snapped.

'You can sit beside Baimbo,' she said, pointing.

The boy looked around the room and walked as slowly as possible down the aisle. Baimbo was delighted. This boy was fearless. He knew they were going to become great pals. The boy stood for a moment at the desk and looked at Baimbo before sliding into seat next to him.

'Hello,' whispered Baimbo, 'Everyone calls me Snailbait.'

The boy was too busy opening his beautiful leather briefcase to reply. Baimbo envied his uniform. The collar was soft, the shirt smooth. He wasn't going to itch all day.

'Miss,' said the boy, closing the briefcase.

'What is it now?'

'Have we got any cabbage remover?'

'Cabbage remover?' asked the teacher, waving her spectacles around with an air of puzzlement. 'What on earth is cabbage remover?'

'It's just,' the boy looked apologetic, 'There's a terrible smell of cabbage where I'm sitting.'

Everyone laughed. Baimbo started blushing. The teacher walked down the aisle towards him. Miss MacDonald said, 'Cabbages don't get to sit an exam. They already know their place in the world.'

Everyone laughed again, delighted to find a teacher with a sense of humour.

'It's getting worse, Miss, the smell.'

Miss MacDonald did the worst possible thing. She asked, 'Can anyone else smell cabbage?'

'Yes, miss,' said Carpacius, jumping up.

'Yes, miss,' echoed Naxmanimede.

Miss MacDonald stood over Baimbo and frowned. She sniffed the air. 'Where did you say the smell was coming from?'

'Just below where you're standing, miss.'

The class erupted in laughter. Carpacius and Naxmanimede drummed their hands on the desk. The new boy stood up and took a mock bow. Miss MacDonald quickly restored order without giving the new boy a telling-off. That wasn't right. Nobody made fun of him and got away with it. And this boy could not escape. Baimbo did not waste any time. As the boy took his seat again, Baimbo stamped down with his bad foot on the boy's toes. But the boy was expecting something and pulled his foot away in time. Baimbo vowed to get his revenge at break. He picked up his pencil and stared down at the examination paper.

He really was going to be top of the class in history. The only problem: so was everyone else.

Who defeated the giants at Kildermauchty? Who defeated the dragons at Strath Pen? Who defeated the polar bears at Ghad Mark? Who defeated the dwarves at Seramaya? Who united the lands of Geish, Levenholm, Crimatoll, Rahm, and the Gullanes? Who is the world's only surviving wizard? Who created the world's first water clock? Who built the biggest palace in the world? Who engineered the longest canal, between Bal Tyre and Ardmeachan, in the world? Who invented counting cakes? Who invented the steam bus?

The answer to all these questions was the same two words: Cinter Bassy.

Except the new boy wrote something different. The new boy wrote two words that made Baimbo's heart race.

The new boy wrote: my father.

Caro Ramsay

"Do you mind? I can't manage."

DC Mulholland had not joined the police to cut up chicken salad for damsels in distress. He looked at DS Costello.

"Here, I'll get it for you." Costello sat on the side of the bed, pulling the plate to the edge of the hospital tray, her eyes straying to the clumsy bruised fingers that protruded from the bandage. She thought the skin was going to split under the pressure. She felt sick. "Why do they give you chicken with a blunt knife?" An attempt at humour.

"Why do they give me chicken at all?" said the patient, her voice indistinct through broken teeth.

"I think this chicken trained with Schwarzenegger," Costello sawed the knife back and forth to little effect. "I could ask them to liquidize it."

The patient tilted her head, one eye closed, her eyelashes stuck together like an old cut in soft ripe fruit. She looked at Costello with the other eye.

"Try a bit?"

"Yeah, try a bit," said Mulholland, pacing the floor of the recovery room. There was something here he wasn't quite getting.

The patient picked up a piece of chicken with her bruised hand, not the good one. She popped it into the side of her mouth and stared at the young detective.

He stared back.

She didn't chew.

"You know the fiscal's going on attempted murder." He never took his eyes of the swollen face, now the deep colour of rhododendrons in July, the wires standing proud like twigs.

"Their decision," she said. It was that.. lack of ...lack of something. Mulholland opened his mouth but the patient spoke first.

"How's Sophie?"

"She's fine Claire, been drawing all over your kitchen wall with crayons."

"She's not with him?"

"No, your mum. He's in custody." Costello waved another piece of chicken on the end of the fork. "Kids bounce back."

"Kids bounce," said the patient quietly, looking directly at Mulholland, her fingers prodding the wires that held her cheekbone together, drawing his attention.

Mulholland dropped his eyes, looking at the forearm above the white of the bandage, a weave of lace and lavender.

"Claire?" Costello asked gently. "Do you think he meant to kill you?"

"Yes." A simple word, quietly spoken. The piece of chicken dropped from her mouth. She prodded the gap in her teeth with her tongue. Mulholland could see the dried blood, the staple holding the cut where her teeth had sliced through the muscle.

"I'll get you some soup, you'll never get better on this stuff," said Costello pulling the tray to one side and adjusting the drip. "You never suspected anything Claire? No change in his behaviour?"

Mulholland butted in. "He had never touched you before? He's never had a speeding ticket as far as we can see, never mind a history of assault on women."

"Woman," she corrected, rolling her eye to look at the ceiling.

"Did you not think anything when he came in? He wasn't expected?" Mulholland's voice was sharp.

"And you never go home unexpected? He told me he was at the office."

"The office told us he was going home."

"He told a friend he was going to his girlfriends," said Costello.

"And his girlfriend gave him an alibi," countered Mulholland.

"Yeah right," said Claire.

Costello glared at Mulholland, telling him to back off. Seventeen highly trained officers at the woman and child trauma unit and she gets a Neanderthal like him

"I know coppers look young nowadays but even you don't look like you were born yesterday," said Claire coldly.

Costello smirked.

Mulholland ignored her. "Did you know he was having an affair?"

"He's always having affairs. What was this one called?"

"Lynne."

"Never had a Lynne before."

"You don't know her?" asked Costello.

"I never know them."

"Why didn't you divorce him?"

"I wish I had." She raised her hand to cup her jaw, as if the effort of talking was getting too much. "Now I wish I had. Because of Sophie, I suppose."

"Stay together for the kid. Not the ten bedrooms and the XK8?" said Mulholland,

"You don't have children then?" said Claire.

"He could have divorced you, this violence is a bit extreme."

"He would have lost half. My husband doesn't like to lose anything." She closed her eyes. End of interview.

"We'll leave you, let you know of any developments."

"Can I see Sophie?"

"Better leave it until your face has calmed down a bit, that's what the doctor said."

She opened her eye and looked at Mulholland, he thought he saw a look of triumph. He knew he was being conned, he just couldn't see how.

Costello waited until the door was shut. "I'll kill the bastard," she said sweetly.

"She's not being straight with us."

"We're not exactly being straight with her, are we? She thinks the surgery was a success, poor love. You heard what the surgeon said. You saw what was written in the report."

"If that clip in her brain goes," Mulholland snapped his fingers. "It's good night Vienna."

"He didn't say *if*, he said *when*," said Costello, looking round for a nurse. "And if it's within a year and a day, the bastard is going down for murder."

"I'm not convinced."

"Bloody men." Costello shook her head and disappeared through the swing doors in search of a kitchen.

The blonde watched them go, she smiled to herself. This was better than she could have hoped for. She looked at the chicken pieces chopped on the plate, sawn through, none of them bigger than her thumbnail, innocuous innocent harmless chicken.

But when frozen and swinging on the rope she had tied to the banister, chicken could smash the human skull as easy as crushing an egg. It wasn't rocket science. One push, the chicken on it's rope, a gentle smack on the forearm. Push again, harder, on the shoulder and again, and again, she counted twenty seven. It had taken her half an hour before she went for the big one.

She could remember now the gentle snick as the bone in her cheek snapped, she remembered waking up on the floor, getting to her feet. She had no idea how she untied the chicken, she just remembered concentrating on holding a towel to her face...no blood trail.

Then she phoned the ambulance.

Attempted murder, there was no way he would get Sophie now, no way Lynne would get him now, no matter what that bloody policeman thought.

When she was better, she and Sophie would go out on a picnic, she would get a bottle of champagne, they could have that chicken cooked and cold with salad, celebrate in the fresh air. She looked out the window at the sun, the grass in the hospital grounds was waving at her. She was desperate to get out.

She was desperate to get Sophie to herself, desperate to get Sophie safe.

In fact, she was dying for it.

Carolyn Wylie

Beware the Fury of a Broken Man

Nick was a pleasant man, as pleasant a man as you could ever hope to meet. Walking down the street he smiled at everybody, a large cheery smile that only the stoniest of faces could not respond to. He worked in an office earned a good living, his colleagues when questioned about him were gracious in their replies.

'Nick? Oh yes lovely chap, always so helpful, always smiling never a bad word to say about anybody.'

He was quite a tall man, with dark hair, deep brown eyes. He was always clean-shaven, always smartly dressed, though he shied away from following fashion. He always wore the same clothes; he did not like to draw attention to himself.

He had a wife, Jennifer, a nurse; they had not been together very long, married only just last year. She was ideal, not too outgoing, not too demanding; the perfect wife. They owned a home in the suburbs of the city in which they worked. A modest home; nothing special, nothing out of the ordinary; unmistakably mediocre.

Nick was working today, it was October, the day had been neither warm nor cold, pleasant; no wind blew. Nick waved goodbye to the security man at the desk and walked into the street, besuited, briefcase in hand. He reached his car, it was red, nothing flashy, nothing that stood out in a crowd. The rush hour was in full swing, yet he waited patiently at every tailback and every traffic light. As he proceeded home the sky grew darker and a definite chill hung in the air. Raindrops began to sing their light- smattering tune on the pavement. He reached his street, the lights in his house were on. Jennifer was in, hopefully getting the dinner ready. He opened the door but no smell of cooking reached him, he searched the rooms, Jennifer was in the living room with her feet up.

Within ten minutes, the smell of cooking filled their home, a pan bubbled on the hob, Jennifer lifted it off. She struggled to see the contents through her swollen black eyes and she dabbed her nose with a tissue as it was still bleeding. She carried the pan across the kitchen, with both hands as her dislocated finger throbbed in pain.

After dinner Nick went out for a drink to his local. Whilst there he talked and joked with the regulars: *what a lovely man.* Superficiality does not exist, only ignorance

It Should Have Been Me

The newspaper announcement glares at me in silent mock: nuptials. 'The happy couple tied the knot in a ceremony.....' I can't read anymore it makes me sick. So he has done it, gone and married someone else. It should have been me.

I knew I loved him from day one, ever since I laid eyes on him, those deep dark eyes, that charismatic demeanour, enigmatic and intriguing. Never letting anything out, speaking in a cryptic code that only I could decipher. We met many times but we were never alone, always surrounded by people pushing and shoving, elbowing me out of the way. He used to look over at me, our eyes meeting across a sea of faces, yet almighty surges always broke the bond and I was always carried away. He couldn't find me again.

When others made fun of him I stood up for him, told them that they were misinformed and that he was a genius. He was away for long periods of time, sometimes I never knew where he was, staying up late with other women, spending countless nights in hotel rooms. I began to wonder if I would never see him again. But I loved him and I knew that he would have loved but he was not given the chance, we would have been so happy together if only the world didn't get in the way, but it has come to this – the Rock Star marries the Supermodel. Such a cliché.

It should have been me.

Clive Briggs

Thoughts on a Visit to Glasgow

A black-dressed young man in Govan telling the keys of his mobile phone reminiscent of an elderly Greek lady telling her beads. Both thinking they may have a direct line to someone or another who might be able to help.

A fascinating trip on the Clockwork Orange listening to the Glasgow patter and marvelling on the foresight that started the underground circle long before the modern age thought of the overground. Then motive power was transmitted by a clamp to a moving wire and a large winch did the work. Up the modern escalator and on to the busy city streets in the city centre.

An Asian couple kneeling on the pavement on Argyle Street. Talking and offering food and drink - bottled water - to a begging young Caucasian down and out who was wrapped in a blanket. Reflection of the multicultural city that is developing in 'The Dear Green Place'. The Caucasian was sitting outside Debenham's emporium, adjacent the door, possibly hoping for an overspill of the warmth from within. Dozens of well dressed over fed people hurried past out of the inclement Glasgow weather intent on a search for today's unnecessary sale bargain but nobody saw. The not to be missed-chance of a lifetime syndrome causing momentary blindness for somebody else's need. Was he just a down and out, chancing his luck as a beggar or a fellow human being in some need? Depends on your point of view I suppose.

A magnificent exhibition in the gallery of modern art. Provocative threatening pictures and sculptures that made an impact. An impact that left me feeling uncomfortable and somewhat inadequate and bruised. No doubt it will fade as bruises do.

The gallery was also showing four short evocative art films from an Asian artist under the title Jigar. (Urdu word for friend or lover). Some parts accompanied by Sitar music. Largely set in northern urban rainy Britain. Interesting and different. An event appropriate for a gallery of modern art I believe. Another perspective on our present lifestyle and from a different cultural background. Not critical piece, just seen through different eyes.

An exhibition and shop in the McLellan Galleries selling work by an American artist cried as "The Artist of Light." John

Kincaid is his proper moniker. Paintings of scenes involving water, grass, riverside walks and lit comfortable reassuring dwellings of middle class American suburbia. Generally shown as evening falls on the scene and street lighting casts pools on walkways and reflects in the water, whilst the house windows glow peaceful, secure and warm. Clever but to me rather twee and maybe rather garish. Affect apparently obtained by using a vast number of coats of conventional oil paint on the bright bits, or so I was told by the sales attendant. I wonder, I have my doubts. I was not convinced by the dimming of light in the area of exhibition which enhanced the perceived glow of the picture lights. Interesting work but expensive.

An exhibition near by of the future plans for Glasgow and its further rebuilding. The city is developing and doing so rapidly, in a modern style, whilst still managing to preserve the better aspects of its great Victorian legacy. Details of street art and other tourist publicity available brought to us by the modern magic of a computer database. Courtesy of the city fathers and their team of waged slaves.

An already broken, rather magnificent statue to Donald Dewar stands looking over his city. Glasses away, further curtailing his vision for the city and Scotland. But at least he did have a vision. Modification to the statue probably the result of a Saturday night's close inspection of the bottom of too many glasses by one of the cities inhabitants. However such folk are only a minority group and not seriously important in the scheme of things. They add what might be called a smattering of local colour.

I walk on to the bus station to catch the express bus to my leafy dormitory suburb and away from the high Glasgow Council Tax. Wonderful thing the free bus passes for us older members of the community. Do we really deserve it just as a sort of reward for daring to leave the comfort and safety of our own private tin enclosure? Do we really deserve it?

What a lot Glasgow has to be proud of. It makes you think. Enjoy it. It is great really.

The Dreamer's Lament

There's a sale at Glen Turret;
A clearing of the cellars;
The disposal of old malts,
Source of aromatic peat odours and tartan dreams,
A dispersal of the water of life that served many a generation of
Scottish folk.

The Famous Grouse new owners of the treasure,
Have no space for old sentiments,
In a distillery claimed the oldest of them all.
History scattered in small bottles
For an accountants profit.

Maybe it's for the best,
The bottled dreams of a flavoursome tipple
Spread far and wide.
Passed to the connoisseurs of Scotland and the world
who will treasure it the more.
Sentiment can still linger in the heart of man
when not armoured in his business suit.

A video of the Famous Grouse, now showing
Visitor attraction in the modern style,
Will bring more people to the Glen
searching for a tartan world of make believe.
Will sell a different spirit blend
To suit a modern taste.

But a way of living, a country craft,
Is passing fast from local folk.
As profit seeks English tourist gold the modern way,
And blending replaces a single malt.

Oh! were I a wealthy man,
to purchase this reminder of a way of life.
Its smells and flavours beyond compare,
Distilled and garnered to linger yet
Within a golden bottle of the nose-ed brew,
Rekindling historic dreams of a glorious past.

Red Planet

Dusty red planet, spinning circling, brooding evil
lurking low in the darkening night sky.
Mars bringer of war, closer than for many a millennium,
pass, on your terrible tireless journey.
Spin away to more distant regions of our universe.

Earthbound red party of power,
spinning out of control,
circling waiting to pounce
on those of different view.

Aggressive, belligerent, isolated state,
bringing tumult in others worlds,
Guns, bombs and lies,
debris of a "Christian Democracy"
circling in space.

An asteroid approaches
our earthly haven of sanctity and peace.
A lump of frozen arid space debris,
possible terminator of our trivial power games.
Do we deserve its careless cold caress?

Magnus Quirk

Magnus Quirk was a petite little man. A round faced chubby little chap who generally wore a great big smile. He could often be seen walking through the centre of the town. I say walking but it would be more accurate to describe movement as a scurry.

He moved at great pace, in and out passing the shoppers as if his life depended on being in time for some urgent appointment. Where did he go you may wonder. Few people saw him ever arrive anywhere. That is difficult to understand for he was generally followed by a string of youngsters, mainly boys but not always. They would trail along behind Magnus like some long unwieldy tail and often to the discomfort of more leisurely shoppers or pedestrians intent on looking in the windows of the shops or just strolling along taking the air. There they were, all in a string, scurrying along and bang suddenly the snake had no head. Magnus had disappeared. The boys would stop, look around, search the shops, split into groups and talk to one another but they could never find the least trace of Magnus. It was as if he disappeared into thin air.

What made it more difficult to understand was the way Magnus dressed. His clothing was a mixture from ages long past but always spotlessly clean. Not new apparently but not shabby either and always extremely brightly coloured. He could be dressed in any mixture of colours and styles but one thing you could be sure of, he always wore a hat.

The hat could be flat like a cap, or a trilby or bowler, sometimes even a little woolly thing topped by a contrasting coloured pompon. In the middle of winter, he could occasionally be seen in a deerstalker with the flaps down to protect his ears. Whatever he always wore a hat. On very rare occasions, feast days and the like he could be seen scurrying along wearing a rather battered Tyrolean style headpiece with a great feather set at a jaunty angle.

Below the hat would appear a motley selection of garments. Shirts with ties, cravats or even occasionally open necked. Waistcoats, jumpers, jackets, hacking or ordinary were all to be seen on occasions on Magnus.

Trousers could be slacks or oxford bags, jeans, flannels grey or white, or odd suit trousers but never ever with a matching jacket. On occasion plus fours or plus twos would adorn his little legs. Once after he had not been seen around for a while he reappeared wearing a rather long kilt. It was a great kilt but it did not suit Magnus. He didn't have the legs for it. Not that you could really see any leg. The hem of the kilt came over the knee and over the top of his stockings. All bottomed off as it were by a pair of old fashioned buckled shoes.

Magnus lived in a rather nice flat. It was situated over a charity shop in a busy side street in the heart of the town. The flat had a door that opened directly on to a landing with stairs that led to the street. A second stairway led directly from the flats kitchen down into the shop below. That Magnus owned the charity shop and leased it to the charity with the odd stipulation that he could wear any of the clothes they happened to have in stock was not generally known. He used the shop more like a extended wardrobe than a business premises and in fact since he requested a negligible rent the charity was well pleased with their deal. However he never seemed short of money. In fact he spent his day doing good and helping the needy.

People used to stop and stare as Magnus hurried past. There was something attractive, strange, almost comforting about the little man. He always smiled, waved to people occasionally, seemed at peace with the world yet one felt that something was not quite right. Some strange aura used to surround the little fellow and he rarely spoke.

Any of the children that followed him might have been able to tell you, had anybody bothered to ask, that whatever route he took on his daily journey he always seemed to disappear in the same area of town. It was an area of mean streets with decaying properties of a by gone age, houses now let as bed sits, a few empty dirty looking bars, the occasional shut dilapidated church, disused warehouses and ill kept corner shops. On street corners the occasional unemployed labourer passed his day waiting for the next giro and the opening of the run down hostelry doors.

Magnus was in fact following the instructions from his god. "Report daily to the Church of the Holy Mother. Enter a disused confessional and meditate on the dreadful things you have done. Someday you will be forgiven." He did not really understand these instructions but he knew from whence they came and followed them diligently. He also new that he had to live a quiet gentle life, avoid contact with children and never ever play his flute. This was the part that caused him the real pain. He knew thousands of tunes. Folk tunes, dances, sombre quite melodies. He had played them all in previous lives. But now, no music.

One day he was sitting in the church confessional thinking of his passed lives when a figure opened the door at the other side and a shadowy face appeared in the grill. Was he imagining it? He had only heard the creaking of the door and seen the indistinct face. No footsteps, no swish of cassock. No voice. He knew no priest served this church. The only people who entered were a few down and outs late at night and then only in the worst of weather. It was said locally to be haunted but truth to tell in that area nobody even cared.

Magnus was suddenly aware he was being asked a question.

"Magnus, what do you miss most in this life." a deep cultured voice asked.

"My music. My lovely music" sobbed the little man. Oh I do miss my music"

"You may play again. On condition." said the deep voice.

Magnus's head shot up. "I'll accept any conditions as long as I can play again. Anything."

"Well, no dance tunes or marches, quiet peaceful music only. Music for relaxation, to snooze and gossip to. This music must be played under the trees in the town square. Every evening you have left, you shall play for the amusement of the old folk."

That evening, at the end of a bright sunny day the square was busy. The seats were all occupied by the older citizens of the town telling tales, exchanging gossip or just snoozing.

Magnus found a seat on the corner of a plinth of an old statue that commemorated an old folk legend of the town. Magnus pulled out an old battered flute and shakily at first started to play. It had been a long long time but soon his confidence grew. His old skills returned. Tune after tune, but only soft gentle music, no dances. There Magnus sat and played every fine evening. Word spread and the crowds grew. A week later the square was packed to hear Magnus play. They came in their hundreds from all around. Even from the more isolated mountain villages. He played all summer, week in week out but gradually autumn fell. The trees began to shed their yellowing leaves and people started to wear their coats when they came to listen to the beautiful wistful melodies. One night Magnus stood up at the end of his concert and spoke to the considerable crowd of all ages gathered in the square.

"Thank you friends for being so kind and forgiving me. I'm sorry for the great ill I visited on you fore fathers. I'm sorry, so sorry. Bless you all. I am going now and will not be able to return to you any more." Away he scurried to his flat.

The following morning he was found with a happy smile on his face dead in his bed. Hamelin has never ceased to talk about the little man and his strange haunting music.

Colour in Life

McMaster
Artist of blue trees, blue views, blue hues
Colourist use of primary red,
Producing flower sparkle on a sterile Grecian scene,
Blue world, with a purple chair.
A still life

My trees are green,
My grass and sea is green,
My eyes are also sometimes too green
For my retired life,
Where avarice should play a minor role.

Blue lends distance to a view,
Hills from the valley seen,
Cloud curtain pulled aside,
We glimpse the sky,
Distance added to a universal world.
In this life.

Why then does my mind accept blue trees?
In an Hebridean scene
Not many trees adorn that windy shore, non blue,
But does a sea of flags
Waving yellow in the sun
Change blue to green?
In the painters life

To pose a question,
Provide no answer
Is this the artists role?
Give paintings names,
Clues for a seeking mind
For my life

Standing Stone

Lichened stone guardian of a Celtic world,
Dominant Lord of all around,
You saw Christianity appear and thrive
Standing silent by day and night.

No prate, no thought, just a presence,
Powerful, free, standing serene,
Symbol of a meditational calm,
Influenced not by human kind.

Visitors now in greater number come,
Pilgrimage made easy in a mobile world,
Can you provide surety and peace,
Menhir of a magic age?

Will any worshipping at your craggy shrine,
Be influenced by your brooding calm,
Take time out from their hectic life,
To consider the example set.

Or are we all in frantic dance
on self destruction bent,
Will we not learn the greater truths?
Of life continued in this verdant glen.

In ages yet beyond the ken of man,
Will you still stand silent and serene,
To be guardian of a barren land,
Wrecked by man's Almighty hand.

The Fisherman's Autumn

A lifetime ago a restless boy brought string and bent pin to the
river,
Offered crusts and brandling worms to the sprite of early
spring.
The fast flowing stream of turbulent winter melt carried the
bobbing
swirling offering to the Gods,
Hope filled eyes sparkled in the hard light
Searched for the greedy grab of young fish.
Bright green spring awoke the sullen, still slumbering earth,
Snow receded on the hill as the young sun god gained strength
For the season yet to be.

In grey headed autumn
The fisherman slowly wades up stream
The long lazy cast of fly and line
Lure and tempt the dozing fish
A swirl and tug and tightening
another squirming bundle of silver clad muscle basket bound.
The last day of the season.
Evening settles still over river and country
A ghost rises and drifts in the cool air
Shrouding the drooping willows in mourning
The purple hills reflect the call of the arrogant bellowing stag
as roseate lights spots the crags
The river merges into the evening grey.
Winter chills creep into the old anglers bones
As he slowly reluctantly heavy footed leaves the river bank.
All life prepares to welcome the reign of the dark Lord.

The wheel still grinds on its bumpy road
with an even pace,
All heaven can rejoice in the annual miracle.
The old fisherman may yet again be reawakened by a new light
Or replaced by a younger body,
The spirit will go on.
String and lines still be cast into water and greedy bodies grab
Whilst wily old fish use honed caution
This is the miracle.
Rejoice in it and worship-

Each in his own way, time and place.

Eleanor Jeffrey

All Hallows' Eve

Three friends who were interested in paranormal phenomenon decided that, for research purposes, they would spend Halloween in a place reputed to be haunted. They advertised in various newspapers and on the Internet and received thousands of letters and email from all over the country, before finally settling on a place that really fired their imagination. It was an ancient castle-like fortress in the borders of Scotland that had been un-occupied for aeons and the boys were delighted when the owner answered their advert and arranged to meet them at his cottage in Ayrshire a few days later. The boys were a bit taken aback when they arrived at the address the owner had given them as the cottage looked derelict and the garden very over-grown but the door opened to their knock and a wizened old gentleman beckoned them in. The inside of the cottage looked as derelict as the outside and the boys looked around in amazement as the owner introduced himself and shuffled to a scruffy old armchair, telling them to sit down while he explained about the castle. About an hour later he leaned forward, eyes glowing eerily and asked if they still wanted to visit the place and, when they nodded excitedly, he pointed a long gnarled finger at them and said they were mad to stay overnight, as it was a vile, evil place. Chuckling mirthlessly he agreed that they could carry out their research and, giving them directions to the castle, he wished them well and waved them on their way.

With their preparations finalised and the equipment all packed, the young men set off early on the morning of Halloween to give them plenty of time to settle in when they arrived. It was a dull but dry day and their journey was uneventful, although the last leg was quite a drive along narrow winding roads over a bleak moor.

The castle sat on a small hill surrounded by a circle of oak trees and was of dank grey stone and half in ruins. The lads were thankful to see that they could shelter in the part that was still standing and unloaded all their electronic gear and sleeping bags. When they had finished they decided to explore, knowing their belongings would be safe as there was no-one around for miles. Taking care where they walked and all carrying their storm lamps, they wandered around the musty rooms and basements and all jauntily agreed that there was an eerie feel to the place.

As darkness fell they lit all the lamps they had brought with them and built a fire in one of the massive fireplaces, using broken branches from the huge oak tree growing at the back of the castle. It was oddly comforting sitting in front of the fire watching the sparks fly up the chimney while eating their sandwiches and drinking bottles of lager. The "Ghost Busting" equipment they had borrowed from their University was all set up and they were eager to use it. It was going to be a real hoot they said as they joked and laughed.

They were starting to get a bit bored as a few hours had passed with nothing happening and they decided to move all their equipment down to a large dungeon like room in the basement. When everything was set up, they lit many candles, switched off the storm lamps and settled down in the mouldy dampness to maintain their vigil.

After an hour or so all the candles snuffed out, plunging them into impenetrable darkness. Startled, the boys grabbed their equipment and jumping to their feet, crowded together with their backs to the wall. The temperature plummeted dramatically, as the sound of soft slithering seemed to come from every corner of the room. The noise filled their heads as an overwhelming stench of decay assaulted their nostrils. As goose-bumps covered their skin and the chill assaulted their bones, the boys snapped instructions to each other as they wrestled to get their "Ghost Busting" kit working and re-light one of the lamps, but the flare from the match revealed something that no nightmare could have done justice to.

A few yards in front of them, a manacled woman stretched her gnarled bony hands towards them in silent plea. As she did so, her rotten rags of flesh slipped from her skeleton and the wisps of long silvery hair still clinging to her whitened skull, blew in their own breeze. As the match sputtered out, a shriek cascaded over the boys, threatening to stop the very blood in their veins. The apparition's screams grew louder and louder and were met with deafening shrieks of unearthly joyless laughter.

The boys clung together, each of them filled with unspeakable horror as unseen icy hands touched at their faces and breathy voices whispered malignant words in their ears.

Petrified, they abandoned their equipment without a thought and stumbled blindly through the darkness towards what they hoped to be the doorway. As they did so, bony fingers plucked at their hair and clothing as they fled up the stairs and their screams mingled with those of the manacled woman, as screeches of depraved laughter followed them out into the dark night.

With hearts thumping and all sweating profusely, they bolted for the safety of their car, as the suffocating presences bore down on them. With his hands shaking uncontrollably one of the boys at last managed to open the car doors and they all fell onto the seats, dragging the doors closed behind them. They expected the car to stall, but instead the engine powered into life as their dreadful tormentors rocked the vehicle from side to side and banged mercilessly against the car's body. The two passengers cursed at their friend who sat rigid with fear behind the wheel, moving him to slam his foot down hard on the accelerator and finally the car screeched down the overgrown driveway and hurtled out onto the road like a vehicle from hell.

The tyres burned as the car hurtled on through the night and did not stop, until the lights of the small village the boys had passed through earlier that day flashed past. The boys were amazed to discover that it was still only nine o'clock. Shakily they left the car and set off to find the nearest pub to calm their nerves. They would also have to find somewhere to stay that night.

They entered a cosy looking inn and ordered some beers from the barman who peered at them and asked if they were alright, as they looked a bit green round the edges. They related their sorry tale to him and he listened in silence until they were finished. Laughing, he told them that it was a wonderful tale for All Hallows' Eve and shrugging his shoulders said that he'd never heard of the place and he'd lived in the area all his life.

Puzzled, the boys looked at each other and then asked the barman if he could be mistaken. Looking askance at them he responded by calling out to the customers, all locals, asking them if they had heard of the castle, but the murmured responses and shakes of various head heads, told them that no-one had.

The boys stayed the night at the Inn and the next day sheepishly asked the local Vicar if he would accompany them back to the castle, as they had to collect their belongings. They told him their story and, perplexed, he agreed to go with them. They left the village and took the narrow winding road over the moors, heading back to that place of horror. But they couldn't find the castle! It had vanished.

Eventually they found the circle of trees where they knew the castle had stood and were absolutely stunned to find all their belongings neatly stacked under the huge oak, as if waiting for them?

The vicar commiserated with them and told them that strange and inexplicable things can happen in this world and that he believed they had seen something weird, as they seemed to be genuinely scared. He wished them a safe journey home when they dropped him back at the village and, shrugging his shoulders, waved good-bye as they drove off.

Safely back at the university the boys never mentioned their horrifying experience to anyone as they could find no trace of their correspondence with the old man nor the map he had given them and the Ayrshire cottage turned out to be an empty, derelict old ruin.

Strangely, their equipment had not recorded a single thing. It was bad enough being haunted, but to be haunted in a non-existent castle they agreed was the absolute pits. Needless to say, they never went ghost hunting again.

The Moon Dance

One night long ago three brothers were fishing on Loch Duich in the Scottish highlands. It was a long night and the fishing was poor when suddenly the youngest brother cried out and pointed to Eilean Donan Castle. The castle sat on a little island out in the loch and the brother pointed to strange lights moving around on the shore below the castle. Abandoning their fishing the brothers decided to investigate and rowed their small boat very quietly across the loch and anchored it near the island.

Creeping across the bridge that joined the island to the main shoreline they hid behind a tree and watched several ethereal and strangely beautiful people dancing on the sandy shore below them, some with flaming tallow torches in their hands. As they watched, the moon came out from behind a cloud and bathed the scene in shining silver. Who were these people dancing and laughing in the moonlight? Gasping in astonishment the eldest brother pointed to the water at three seals that had come ashore and as they watched in amazement the creatures cast off their fur skins and became three maidens who rushed across the sand to dance happily with the others. *They were the seal people. The Selkies.*

The brothers had heard the legends of the creatures that cast off their fur skins and take on the likeness of humans and they knew that some of them married mortals but were seldom happy on land and returned to their homes beneath the waves. It was said that if a mortal could steal the selkie's skin while it was in human form he or she was the master over the true owner, as the seal could not return to the sea without its skin.

The brothers knew it was unwise to get involved with the seal-people. They had heard the Selkie stories all their lives and knew it could be dangerous but were so enchanted by the three beautiful seal-maidens they had watched coming out of the water, with their knee length shining black hair and pearly white bodies, that they decided to steal their fur skins.

The dancers were so engrossed in their dancing that they didn't notice the brothers sneaking onto the shore and snatching the skins until it was too late! Immediately the seal-people stopped dancing and tried to catch them but the brothers were like quicksilver and escaped with the skins.

Tragically this meant that the seal-people had to return to their homes beneath the water and abandon the girls to their fate.

The seal-maidens begged and pleaded and cried to be set free when the brothers claimed them for their wives but it was only the youngest brother who returned his maiden's skin. He was so moved by his beautiful maiden's distress that he returned her skin and watched broken-hearted as she swam away. The other brothers happily married their maidens and set up home.

Weeks passed before the seal-people returned again at the full moon and found the youngest brother sitting on the shoreline overwhelmed by grief, calling for his lost love. The seal- father of the maiden felt sorry for the young mortal and told him that his daughter had fallen in love with him and, because the young man had been kind to her he would allow them to meet on the shore every time the moon was full. The young man was delighted when his beautiful maiden, with her long, coal black hair billowing around her, ran into his arms and they danced joyfully in the moonlit shadow of the eerie castle.

Unfortunately the other brothers did not fare so well.

The middle brother kept his poor Selkie wife a prisoner and would not listen to her pleadings to go home. She loved him but missed her mother and sisters and thought he was cruel to keep her hidden away. Alas, he was careless one day and forgot to lock the large box he kept in the attic where he had secreted her fur skin. When she found it she ran to the loch and quickly disappeared beneath the waves.

Chasing after her he stood at the water's edge and broken-heartedly calling her name, he begged for forgiveness and pleaded with her to return to him. Suddenly her head appeared through the water a few yards off shore and she began to sing in a high sweet voice and beckoned to him. Bewitched he walked into the water and was quickly trapped by the other seal-people and taken to their home deep in the loch where he was now *their* prisoner, never to be seen again.

The eldest brother loved his wife very much and tried to make her happy. He bought her beautiful clothes and worldly goods but, alas, the poor creature was missing her seal friends and family and became sad and pitiful. When this brother heard what had happened to his middle brother he was worried his wife would find her fur skin and disappear beneath the waves too. Desperate to stop this happening he decided to burn the skin and built a huge bonfire at the back of their cottage on a cold autumn night and, when the fire was red-hot, he threw the skin onto it and watched it sizzle and sputter.

Realising what he was doing his delicate little wife rushed out of the house distressed and screaming and tried in vain to rescue her seal skin but accidentally fell into the flames and was killed. The distraught man was un-consolable for months and eventually went mad with grief and took to wandering the surrounding hills searching for her.

For a long time people talked in hushed voices about the three unfortunate brothers, who did not heed the warnings about the Selkies. Legend has it that when the moon is full you can see the youngest brother and his seal-maiden dancing on the sandy shore below Eilean Donan Castle and, if you look out over the loch you might see a strange splashing and hear a faint cry that sounds vaguely human. Also on clear, cold autumn nights you may see a ghostly ragged man with a long beard wandering the moon-silvered hills calling for his lost love in a high thin voice that echoes eerily down the glens.

G.I. Campbell

A Society of Snow

The tenement house lies
Ugly and ruined inside
Its old and dirty face
With windows that are eyes
The door makes a wooden nose
Wardrobes lacking in second hand clothes
Dusty shelves of stinking food
It reeks poor and crude

The villa contrasts
A beauty while it lasts
Smooth, painted surface
Pollution free; now safe
Windows; curtains clean
No richness is left unseen
Plated with character
Drawn with hope

Now in the winter
When snowflakes fall fast
They provide a cover
To hide all the contrast
Everything a beauty
Buried by purity
Everything becomes unknown
Nothing is certain in a society covered in snow

Dead Star

Our love
We were a star in the night
Studied by star gazers
Everyone
To them a dot in the sky
No one really understood
They just observed and made
Stories. Maybe phoney
But we didn't care
Envied even by time

Our love
Flickered like a failing light
A black hole was born
We became a dead star

Lord Have Mercy On Us

Signs show on the skin
Black as death itself
Buboes in the groin
Head splitting: tongue swells

I've walked in London
I have felt the air
Felt 30,000 claimed souls
Pleading for their freedom
Burning of blood in their homes

Lord, have mercy on us
Condemned behind a blood red cross
The husband's fate known
The family must share his destiny
A baby's cry locked in
Left to perish as if for sin

Charles flees his home
His courts closely follow
For the poor he has no care
They're left imprisoned
Penniless is their crime
A posy: their only defense
By the wealthy they are condemned

The Devil's Gate

When the spirit seeps through
Your skin. The pain is replaced by
Emptiness. Silence; nature just hisses
Taunts.
Shortly; funeral bells
Who wants to live forever?

The spirit steadily drifts like
A seagull in calm wind
Slowly, it approaches a waiting room
But first stands the set of gates
Blood red gates
Devil gates
All desire faded; greed now dead

Crying as they open, the
Gates moan – then
Screaming as they painfully close
Behind the wandering spirit that is
Now a lifeless white
Cold and shuddering; in the
Warmth of hell

Not alone; now amongst other
Spirits. All of sameness
Deathly. Horribly starved of
Life.
Sucked of colour; blood trembled
Inside. Like an earthquake
Spirits – tearless; Human's desire

Fiona Lindsay

Nothing Special

The landlady is large, Polish and alcoholic. We stand in my room, my holdall and case on the floor at our feet, while she tells me about the long ago political ructions which led her to escape Warsaw and the Polish authorities, and eventually end up in this West of Scotland town. She speaks in slurred, heavily accented English, and I presume she's told this story many times before, but it diverts me for a few minutes. She is hazy with vodka and shows no curiosity. She calls me Lucille, because I asked her to, even though I have never liked it and only ever used it for filling in forms. My surname was changed twice, on my mother's second marriage and my first, but now I've gone back to my original name, the one on my birth certificate, which is at the bottom of my holdall, creased and yellow.

The landlady shuffles off to her own part of the house and I am left alone. The room is small and L-shaped, with a heavily patterned carpet and walls painted a greying white. I plan to buy a couple of posters, maybe some cushions. There is a narrow, cheap wardrobe and chest of drawers, a bedside cabinet, a wash hand basin which emits ghostly sounds, a kettle sitting on a low table and a big bed. It looks ancient but is surprisingly comfortable when I sit on it. I start to unpack, but it only takes a few minutes: my documents, some food hastily grabbed from the kitchen, toothbrush and soap, clothes chosen for practicality and comfort. The wardrobe rattles with plastic and misshapen wire hangers when I open it. I arrange the tins and packets of food along the table, and put a small radio by the bed. Then I look around. There is evidence of previous tenants here and there - a pale brown patch on the wallpaper where coffee has been flung, telling of an argument, in a drawer a postcard from Venezuela, and a decapitated doll. Now everything is unpacked I don't know what to do. It is only mid-afternoon. Nobody knows I am here. My mobile phone sits on the kitchen table, back at the house. I walk over to the window and look out. It's a busy main road and people walk by. It rumbles with buses and cars. There are a few pubs, an off-license and a bookmaker, and, incongruously for this part of town, a Mediterranean cafe, which doesn't seem to have any customers. There is no sound from the rest of the house. I guess my new landlady has passed out.

I decide to make some tea. Now that I've thought of it I'm desperate for its warmth and comfort, desperate for the familiarity of the ritual of making it. Water, milk, tea bags. I look hopefully at the groceries I brought: half packet of cornflakes, tins of soup and baked beans, dried milk, hard bread and marge, but no tea bags. I put on a jacket and go downstairs, blinking as I emerge from the darkness of the close into the daylight. Only my pressing need for tea makes me go on. I feel exposed outside. I chose this town because I'd only been here once, as a teenager. We'd come here on a school trip because it was famous for weaving and a poet who killed himself. We'd wandered around the museum and some preserved weavers' cottages, whispering and giggling, not especially interested but enjoying the treat of a day out of the classroom. Still, it stayed with me and I remembered the name. It's a big town, big enough for me to merge into the crowd. It's tagged onto the south side of the city, the opposite part from where I grew up.

Everything is new to me as I walk along, scanning the shop fronts. This heightened sensitivity makes me feel vulnerable, as if everyone is looking at me, although really I know they are not. I am nondescript - small, brown haired, approaching middle age. My clothes - jeans, trainers and anorak, made me look like any local woman. My face is clear, except for a small scar just above my left eyebrow, which won't go away, but I can always put it down to a childhood fall. I could be anyone. Outside the grocer's three women stand chatting, one with a baby in a pram, and I think that one day this town will be my home, and people will no longer be strangers.

I used to wonder in the beginning why Jonathan was attracted. I didn't really measure up. But he chose me and I was ecstatic. We were married and I had at last my dream wedding. I didn't understand why he could be jealous, sometimes, of a girl as ordinary as me, but I liked it, in a way. It showed he could be passionate, that he cared.

The grocer's shop is run by two Indian men who talk in their own language while I walk around. It is packed to the roof, leaving only narrow aisles. I locate the tea bags at the back of the shop, the milk beside them. The shop assistant barely glances at me as I pay for them. He hands me my change and goes back to his conversation. I clutch the bag against me and jog back to the flat. It is still in silence. An old fashioned phone sits on a table in the hall, but no one I know has the number. Most of my friends had given up on me, anyway. *You've got to leave him, Lucy, please,* they'd say, increasingly desperate and exasperated.

I push into the room again, and it looks no less depressing than when I went out, but it is mine and it is quiet. I fill the kettle at the wash hand basin, plug it in and wait for its whoosh and click. I drop a tea bag into my mug and splash the boiling water over it. The scent of the tea rises and I sniff it appreciatively. I stir in some milk and hold up the mug. *Cheers,* I say to the empty room.

James Carruth

Angel

For the death of others
he waits on gate posts

or scars the sky above
soaring slow wide circles.

His wind ruffled furrows
hung high on crucifix wings

marking the frosted shroud
of moor and ploughed field,

small streams trickle
below the grip of ice.

Hawk eyes
scour the silence

for a faintly stirring,
heartbeat ball of fur,

finds hunger soft-pawed
in open ground

stranded far
from sanctuary.

In a rush of air
calls down a liturgy

of buzzard thrust
and blackthorn claw

curved beak rip
cracks gravity

through boned flesh,
eclipses day.

The Daughters of Proetus

"Don't send me any more cow poems" Sally Evans, *Poetry Scotland*

How can I possibly stop now
My muse will not let me
For the nectar of milk is my wine

So I'll bow down drunk again
At the shrines of bucolic beauty
Show-day daughters of Proetus

With clippered top lines
Tail perm perfections
Parading pride as the prize

Through a June heat haze
Graceful manicured hooves
Haltered heads and red rosettes

Haughty heifers of Holstein
Hold high your gleaming muzzles
Stretch necks to graze the sky

Bovine goddesses of milk
Shiny hides silken and pied
Swinging those glorious udders

Oh princesses of talcum powder
Your black has never been so dark
Your white has never been so light

Our ladies of the long lactation
Succours of this once great nation
Accept again my humble praise.

* the daughters of Proetus were punished for their pride by being
made to believe they were cows

The Progressive Canadian Barn Dance

The first time she wore the new dress
was at the farmers' harvest dance
on a night breathless and warm.

Uneasy with her body's new bloom
she would have sat the night out
had her mother not dragged her up

to be thrown around like a doll
from rough hands to rough hands
from Anderson to Macgregor

from Macgregor to young Wilson,
in his father's tight tweed jacket,
from Wilson to club foot Brogan

from club foot Brogan to Lamberton
and his scabby working bunnet
from Lamberton to the moleman

from the moleman to his apprentice
staring at her in his strange way
from the apprentice to Patterson,

who danced fast but talked slow,
from Patterson to Uncle Jack
not her real uncle of course

He held her too close and grinned
told her how much she'd grown up
she struggled free from his grip

found one of the Mackenzie boys
from one of them to the other,
with their shiny new market boots,

and on to old Wilson with his crook
and on to his buddy Baxter
smelling of his black face flock

from his strong stench to Anderson
scratching his ringworm
from Anderson to Macgregor

who birled her until she was dizzy
from Macgregor to young Wilson,
they say he'll never be his father,

from Wilson to Brogan's brown eyes
from brown-eyed Brogan to Lamberton
who throws his bunnet onto a seat

she grabbed him, the pace quickened,
the dance lifting her dress up light as air,
she spun him away before moving on

to Lamberton then the moleman
sweating lochs through his winter shirt
after the moleman his apprentice

from the cross-eyed apprentice
to big Patterson flustered and red
from Patterson on not to Uncle Jack

who has retired wheezing to the bar
but the clumsy Mackenzie boys
taking turns to bruise her feet

before passing her to old Wilson
who staggers to keep up with her,
tells her he once courted her mother

Oh surely not she laughs out loud
winks at him in a new confidence
then glances back at her mother

then on to his drinking pal Baxter
from his beery breath to Anderson
from Anderson to Macgregor

from Macgregor to young Wilson
from Wilson to Johnny Brogan
he clasped her hand tight, echoed

her smile and the music stopped.

My wife becomes a field

It started in bed
a couple of new shoots sprouting from her navel;
something fungal, best not to mention,
but it spread so quickly
down her thighs along her arms,
transforming her back into a turfed lawn.
It tickles she laughs, puts down her book.
In her meadow sweet breath
she boasts of deep roots, broad leaved foliage
shows off a greening body:
a new outfit of rampant vegetation,
but I'm no gardener, and anyway
you can't take a set of shears to your wife.
I chew on a blade of fescue,
explore the rolling hills of her breasts,
hedges form along each rib;
fingers blossom from branches into trees.
Gathering up her hair in handfuls of clover,
I gaze below tufted flower beds to each iris:
a cluster of harebells dancing.
Blowing on her neck
I launch a million dandelion clocks
across fertile valleys.
In an hour she takes our bed
from Winter to full blown Summer,
disappearing under her own pasture.
Through head high grass I follow,
falling and reaching out for warm earth.
Beneath my nails seeds germinate and grow.

Barnbeth

I.

Daytime
Barnbeth Loch
carries bonspiels
on its back,
empties the village.
Curlers lunge
like swordsmen,
red-nosed children
wedged in wellies
waddle and fall hard.
The guttural rumble
of granite
drowns all.

II.

Fitful sleep
pervades my night.
One dream,
an unnamed man:
brooding weight
encased in ice.
I fill his life
with stories
stolen from myths.
I want him
to open his eyes,
from black lips
speak truths.

III.

Decision
shudders me awake,
dresses me,
drags me back
to Barnbeth -
blinking skywards

at dwindling echoes
of dead language,
crunching snow fields
under foot,
my breath a second skin.
I break through
the elm ring
guarding the loch
like a miser's coin,
to stand
on solid light
at the edge of words.

IV.

Close to the centre
I drop prone
on to thinning ice
hearing
for the first time
straining timbers,
a tightening
under the hull,
ancient voices
struggling in a silver wake,
wind whispering
a fragile flurry
across the loch
a promise.
My fingers,
skeletal chills
in numb gloves
trace the calligraphic arcs
of skaters,
intricate striates
on an ice lexicon.

V.

I face the trapped:
bubbles,
pond weed,
pale grasses
filigree of fern,
speckled trout -
a silhouette
becomes
the stranger
from the dream,
his face
my own.

VI.

I pummel the lens

for a pulse
beneath,
the blood
of words
seeping up
dark towards
the glass
that cracks,
shatters.
I grasp
through shards
for the gargle
of new vowels,
reply in tongues.

Island Rhythms

Exoduuusss
Movement of Jah people
Is what he sings unaccompanied
In the karaoke at Stornoway
For though he asks for Jimmy Cliff,
Toots and the Maytals,
All they ever have is
Blanket on the Ground;
And his Reggae Ceilidh band
Bob Mackintosh and the Whalers:
With their self-proclaimed mission
To bring rhythm and bass
Back into the heart of the psalms
Lasted only one gig
Old Miss Munroe from the post office
Less than pleased to be asked
To take her partner for some lovers' rock
Constable Macleod shocked too
By Bob's confession that he'd shot a sheriff.
However his crocheted reggae hats
Have been an unexpected hit
As working bunnets for crofters across the island
Each its own tiny rainbow
Between overcast skies and bog;
And on Sunday afternoons when it's dry

A small band of loyal followers
Gather to hear him and smoke peat spliffs.
He tells them they're all Africans
Promises the return of Haile Selassie
But does not give a ferry time.
With his hair splayed out in the wind
More matted cow tail than dreadlock
He skanks around the standing stones
Chanting to himself an incantation
I an' I - Wee Free Rastafari,
I an' I - Wee Free Rastafari.

Kalashnikov's Mower

"I would have preferred to invent something which helps people.
A lawn mower for example"

Mikhail Kalshnikov (82)
inventor of the rifle named after him

Later
you will boast
of the prototype
to the neighbour,
who leans over the fence
a witness,
wheel it from the shed
point out
features of note
drive shaft
half pulley
gear case
blade cover
recoil assembly
the gas return tube
above the barrel
a long box magazine
handle like a trigger
all made from materials
just lying around.
It is amazing
what can be done
when you
put your mind
to it
You comment
on its ruthless
accuracy,
rounds per minute,
but not the flutter felt
as you flicked
off the catch.
Pulse and rhythm
became you

breathing in
first the machine,
with time
the reek of cut grass,
the fallen,
mown down
in swathes,
evidence of its power.

Machair

and it was the way
you said the word makar

as you eulogised
in the hushed silence

of a coastal church,
submerging old Scots

with the lilting undertones
of your island voice

that helped me picture
each poet who ever lived

as one grain of sand
on a Hebridean beach

together responding
in constant wonder

to changing winds
and lunar tides

forever shaping
new verse.

Old Ploughman

Davidson staggers home
past the village school:
a boarded-up shell
whose bell used to echo
the old smiddy's spark
while inside the headie
belted the quiet and dumb.
Beyond the orange glow
of the last street light
his progress becomes
a dark uneven furrow
each gate on his way
is a resting point
closed on the past.
There was a time
he could have tilled
the stars into line.
Beneath
the untended Plough
he stops to listen
to an overture
across stubble fields:
a dog bark,
a hungry bellow,
a tractor started up
ready for the day;
his hands rattle
the barred gate:
a quiver of ploughshare
against hard rock.
Letting go at last
he sets off again
through the dawn,
his old markers
stations of the cross.

Roddie Bain (Ruairidh Aili Dhuibh)

Half a century ago
against a big sky
Roddie Bain
ageing acrobat
in waistcoat and cap
balances in worn boots
along the side of
a wooden wheel barrow
performs with poise
for an audience of one;
master of rutter and tusk
he teeters on the edge
to lay one last peat
atop the dark stack
willing to risk,
for his art,
a summer fall
to warm
his winter bones.

Tattie Howker's Daughter

in my voice
not theirs

I searched for words
to name you

and found them in
small hawk's shadow

cob's ragged mane
blaze of gorse

blackthorn thicket's
sweet bloom and sloe

sinews of cirrus
thistledown

ripening barley
blast flattened

by their coarse gusts
Filthy Midden Tink.

Welcome

And she
who still leaves
the back latch off
despite our pleas,
prepares
for any visit
unannounced
with sandwiches
and a small churn
covered with
a cotton table cloth
does not see
the travellers
as trouble makers
murderers or thieves
or even as princes
or troubadours
but simply
distant cousins
There but for the
her oft quoted mantra
lost on us.
Today
when we show up
she is shaking
her head
at the paper
tutting at Dungavel
It's not right
Not right at all.
There's a proper way
to welcome strangers:
as one of your own
Not convinced
I fully understand
she repeats it
One of Your Own

John Coughlan

Craich

1000 hrs

The blank page mocked him. Slightly damp, it lay on his knee. Brian held a cheap biro clenched in his fist to thaw the ink. You would think a man on the edge of everything could think of something to say to his wife, to his child. One last message in case things went pear shaped. In case things went arse up. Words of care, love, sorrow even, but nothing came. Sitting on his gear with his unloaded rifle lying across his thighs, he stared out from under the edge of the wind snapped poncho, his mind numbed and empty as he watched the beads of rain and sleet pelting down the gully to the west. A watery sun glowed weakly, a soft haze with no warmth. He cooried deeper into his maggot bag. He would never feel warm again. Something with lots of legs was inside his helmet, feeding off the dirt and sweat in his scalp.

Down the gully the 105's were flinging their shells over the ridge onto the Argie positions on the south slope of Two Sisters. A puff of smoke and a flash at the muzzle, the gun dancing lightly in the pit to the soft tinkle of brass and the muted orders of the gun layer. A heavy door slammed shut, announcing their arrival on target. They should have a sign up, 'Danger! Men at Work!' God help anyone lying under that. The rest of the company were dispersed along the walls of the cut. Some had rigged communal shelters and were hunched together pooling the last of their fags and nutty. Here and there a furtive bottle of Navy rum was passed around the magic circle.

It wasn't fair. He was too tired to write, and if it all went wrong what would it matter?

The warning order had come up in the night from Ajax Bay. They'd been withdrawn from the sodden peat holes where they crouched among the flint crags just below the Argie positions and moved in the night two klicks back down the gully. Roused after five hours sleep they'd eaten their first hot food for three days then gathered in the sheep pens and told. The orders were stark. Nobody said anything or looked at anyone else. They were to carry out a night infantry assault in battalion strength at 2300 hrs, up the southern ridge of Two sisters and storm the enemy positions. They would be first company up and would be supported by 81mm mortars and the artillery of 29 Commando Battery, carrying the position with the bayonet. Easy for them to say, they weren't fucking going. Fucking simple. Piece of Pish. Eezy Peezy. Just Tora Peachy. Jesus Weeping Christ.

The empty page still mocked him.

Down the slope he saw Crawford, the company runner, slogging up the muddy slope through the steaming clumps of men, head turning and searching. Preying fucking mantis! He was looking for him Brian knew and he sat unmoving and silently waited. Every second ticking by was a jewel. He lit a bent fag and watched Crawford come. Let the bastard work for it. Crawford paused and spoke to one of the rum drinkers, who turned Judas and pointed up to where Brian was holed in. Crawford was breathing like an iron lung when he reached him. He stuck his rifle butt in the slope as an anchor and struggled to speak. Brian blew smoke in his face until Crawford recovered enough to rest one hand on his knee.

"What wonderful bloody news do you bring?"

"Section and Troop Oic's briefing at 1200 hrs," Crawford gasped. "Got any nutty or fags?"

"Naw! Where?"

"Company HQ, just behind the gun line. Sheep pen."

"That figures. Are they giving us lunch?"

"Awe Aye! Full buffet. Got nay dry gear, gash socks like?"

"Naw! Find some other sucker."

Crawford wasn't to be put off. "Fraser telt me you had socks spare."

"Fuck off! You can have them off my cold dead feet."

1200 hrs.

The shearing shed was packed and the air was tropical with the sweat and damp of the men, packed like sardines into the shed. Captain Taylor moved along the corrugated wall and stood perched on a tubular steel rail.

"Right! Bit of hush now. Listen up. We don't have much time and I don't want to hang about here. One stray mortar round could seriously stimulate promotion in HQ company."

He scanned the press of men. "Davie Munro! Where are you?"

Brian's troop commander struggled to raise his hand.

"Ah right! I see you now. I want your boys up at the start line by full dark. Since you lot have already reccied and know where all the nasty surprises are, you can be first and lead us all in."

"I'm obliged, sir."

"Have your lead section right up hard by the crags and the minefield in plenty time. Assault engineers will lift prior to 2300 with your lot protecting, but even if they have not finished prior to zero you will still have to commit to the initial assault. You must take the bunker and then hold their total attention. Make their eyes water young Davie."

Brian wondered where they taught officers all this pish. Munro nabbed him as he tried to slink out.

"Start the men on prep Sgt; I'll be up around 1400 to do a model brief."

Brian nodded and slogged back uphill towards the bivvy. The guns had switched fire missions and he could hear the mortar fire speeding up. Choppers were dropping under slung ammo loads at the gun line.

"Fire faster, you bastards," he muttered.

The bears would be delighted. He found they had moved out of the freezing wind, a gang of tinkers moled, into the earth bank watching some horrible mess bubble in two Dixies and passing a huge pint mug of coffee. Delighted wasn't the word when he gave the order.

"You're fucking kidding."

"Giezzabluidybrekhere!"

"Jesus Limping Christ on a donkey."

"Only a fucking bampot would stick his head up that bloody gully."

"Do they know what's up there?"

"Aye! Two fifty cal, and antitank, and a squad of ticked off Argie Marines in supporting trenches. These guys urnae conscripts boss, they're goin' tae kick the crap out of us, they urnae doin the bunk jist cos we speak roughly to them."

"Stick their bunker up their arse."

Brian let them moan on and wind down till only Fraser was left muttering;

"Fuck! Fuck! Fuck! This gully is going to kill us; we're all going to bloody die."

The coffee came round to Brian. Boiling, strong enough to stand the spoon in, thick with rum and sugar. He gasped.

"We don't need the argies to stiff us; Jones' brew will do that."

Pudsey made a baaa-ing noise and they all joined in and began to laugh.

'*They must be mad,*' Brian thought, '*but who would notice a madman here.*' He shook his head as he remembered someone saying '*if there was a sane man on a battlefield he would leave it.*'

1300 hrs   Prep.

"Okay! Listen up. Gun group, Fraser and Jones. Take the gun and the spare barrel. I want a full strip this pm, and draw fresh ammo. A thousand link belted for instant use on a ratio of five to one for tracer. Red tracer. Take the tool kit and do stoppage drills for one hour. Tamper, comms, so you get to carry the Clansman. Call sign is Zulu 3-4; setting is new, 5-1-2-4. Sterling Smg and ten mags. Soapy, CJ, Pudsey, Tonka, will be rifle group. Each of you will draw a LAWS and four frag grenades; also, one Willy peter each for final clearance."

He was amazed how casually he detailed the tools. Willy Peter or White Phosphorous to the ignorant. Flung into a trench or bunker it would stick to and ignite anything, burning a man to the bone. No amount of water or earth could snuff it. Rumour had it, two Para had shot enemy wounded as a mercy. He continued.

"Each of you will carry two hundred link belted for the gun. Six full mags, last two rounds green tracer, a hundred rounds spare in bandoliers."

He looked up. They were all staring at him vacantly. Expressionless. What were they thinking and what did it matter?

"We'll have arty and mortar support, two SF guns on Longden and close support from a Milan section with two missiles. The Milans will deploy up the gully with us and take the bunker out."

That raised a few smirks.

"They'll have to be better than the fuckwits we saw on Longden then, they were lucky to hit the fucking mountain. Let's hope they've been practising."

Brian smiled, let them laugh.

"Okay, two cooks have volunteered to be ammo carriers, so keep them closed up behind us and hopefully they won't do anything helpful, like step on a mine or trip a flare."

"Are they craphats?"

"Are they stupid mad craphats, John Wayne, gimme a medal?"

Brian let all the dimwit comments wind down until he

had their attention again.

"Heads up! Listen in here. These guys are leaving a safe billet to come up this shitpile and help us take this bunker. Their reasons are their own, but the bottom line is, they didn't have to. Nobody ordered them here. They may not be the soldiers you think you are, but they're going the same place you are because they chose to go. So, respect that."

"Get your brains wired to your arses. I want full and total prep. At dark the assault engineers will begin to clear the left of the gully as much as possible, of trips and mines. Even so, we still have to face and deal with two emplaced fifty cals, an antitank weapon of some sort, grenades, small arms, mortars, the full array of infantry weapons, all operated by regular, motivated, and now thoroughly pissed off Dago Marines."

"If we are not quick and ruthless gents, they will turn the gully into a killing ground."

He had their attention now. CJ Boyle raised a hand.

"I take it then that we, or rather you, have a cunning plan?"

"Mr Munro has."

"Oh aye! We're screwed."

1400 hrs.

Each found a small niche and settled down. Rifles first would be cleaned and wiped free of oil, then the mags would be unloaded and the springs taken out, clearing them of any crud or grass. They would have to load two rounds short, allowing a space at the base of the mags for all the crap to gather, or it would be picked up by the rounds and get into the working parts. A jam was unthinkable. A dry rag would wipe all the damp from the working parts.

Brian applied a light coat of oil, and then reassembled each part with care and precision meshing each with its neighbour. Every round he examined for the slightest deformity or rusted caps, then placed them just so onto the feed tray, the last two rounds were green tracer.

Jones and Tamper came back with the ammo and grenades, and began to divvy them up. With them came a slight spotty boy, stumbling and awkward under his load of ammo liners, eyes wild and wide under a helmet the size of a dustbin lid. He looked like a startled turtle. "Who are you?" Brian demanded.

"Robert Harper, I'm the ammo number for you. I'm a

cook."

'*Christ Almighty*,' Brian thought. He looked as though he were twelve and out for Halloween.

"How old are you, sunshine?"

"Nearly nineteen."

"There were meant to be two of you."

"Well, some of them dropped out after the briefing."

Who said cooks were stupid? He shook his head and took some of the lad's liners. One of the squad asked sarcastically if they could drop out as well and the rest laughed. Brian ignored them, sat back down and nodded at the boy.

"Dump your gear by me and listen up. You keep up with the gun group and the gimpy no matter what. This is Fraser, the long streak of pish Jones there, is his two. You do what they say. No quibble. When they shout for ammo up, you come fast and hard. The only reason you don't come is 'cos you're dead. Do you understand?"

The boy nodded and wormed under the poncho, eyes now wider and fear filled. Fraser passed him the mug.

"Are you good at the cooking young Robert?"

"Aye, no bad. I've got ma City & Guilds. Plan to open my own place some day."

He gulped at the mug and recoiled scalded and poisoned.

"God! Its biling, what the hell is in here?"

"Nothing that will actually kill you." Fraser took the mug back, supped and passed it on.

"You might be an okay cook right enough, but you're going to be a fucking excellent ammo number my son."

1500 hrs.

They moved back down to the sheep pens shortly after and dumped their heavy gear and bergens next to a huge slurry pit. Munro had been a busy little beaver on their behalf. A large Dixie of mutton stew seethed over the fire, and someone had produced real potatoes. Endless hot coffee and chocolate were laid on.

"Hot food and coffee made with milk." observed Jones "must be worse than we thought."

A rough scale model of the attack area was sculpted out of bog and rock. The troop and section commanders squatted at the front and the bears crouched at the rear. Munro hunkered down, using his bayonet for a pointer and began to reveal his cunning plan.

"Right! Listen up! This mess tin is the enemy bunker and its trench system. The two lines of boulders are the sides of the gully. The string is our line of advance and also marks the flanks of our assault. The bits of four-by-two are fire support bases, this scrape is our company start line, red tape is the forward edge of battle or FEB. You have no friends forward of these co-ordinates."

He paused ensuring this had sunk in. They stared back at him, said nothing.

"Right. Enemy forces are known, as is their armament. You can bin all the rumours about Dago conscripts keeking themselves and legging it at the first shot, it's a load of bollocks. These men are regular Marine troops; some of them are 'Buso Tactico."

Groans, moans, hung heads, sharp intake of breath all round, a definite 'nippy sweetie' job this.

"Just fucking peachy." said Tamper.

"That's it noo," said CJ, "Goanae greet noo."

"Ah knew it, Ah just crudding knew it," Fraser muttered into his hands

Munro silenced them, holding up both hands to fend off the racket and shouting, "Mission!" The hubbub died away, silenced by the Clr Sgt and the junior NCOs.

"Mission!" he continued, "M company will carry out an attack up the south ridge and seize the rocky top at height 292. The gully bunker must be neutralised prior to the attack, or it will shred the right flank of our assault. This separate action will be carried out by two section under Sgt Crawford, who has already been briefed. Local support for this will be provided by a Milan team and by sustained fire gimpeys firing from the rear on fixed laser sighting, both tasked to silence the bunker and the fifties. This minor action will be carried out prior to the company action. A surgical strike if you will."

"Hark at him," whispered CJ, "it's us that are goin' tae get surgically bloody struck.

"What does he mean by a minor action?" Robert asked Jones.

"Cos.' they're sending boys weans and halfwits to do it" was the answer.

Munro spread out the tactical map for section commanders to copy details from and took Brian aside.

"I know this is a shit deal for your section after being up the jungle the last two nights, but you have patrolled the gully and know the ground better than anyone. It's essential that this part of the attack is successful. Some bad news I'm afraid; Tac HQ has decided to deploy only one Milan team and not two."

Brian continued writing in his order book, his face expressionless.

"That's nice sir, can you tell me why?" Munro looked embarrassed.

"It's felt that if the team misses or misfires, they won't get time for another shot at it and you will be committed to go anyway."

So there it was then. If they missed on the first go they would all be caught in the open and killed before they closed, unable to assault or escape. He had a mental picture of the twisted Argie dead at Acacia House.

"Not because they cost six grand a whip then?"

Munro chose to ignore that.

"I've given you the best team I have. Mad Alec and his sidekick Ross, if they can't do it, nobody can. You must be at your assault positions in the gully by 2250. At 2255 the Gimpeys will open up in support on fixed lines by azimuth and nitelite. Keep a tight rein on the bears, stay left on your approach, bearing right at the bunker to enter the trench system."

Brian continued to sketch the tactical info on his map. He remembered what his Dad had told him about plans, from when he was second wave at Gold beach. *'Not worth a fart in the wind once the first shot cracks away.'*

Munro continued.

"There is some good news. Eddy the medic has suggested he and his team go with you because of your exposure and it's been okayed by Company."

Brian stuffed his map inside his smock.

"Private health package flung in then, must cancel that BUPA thing. If any more people volunteer we'll probably have to put a bus on."

Munro checked his watch.

"I want you at your start line by 2100. Milan and Medic will RV with you there. For now, get your section back to the harbour area, the Padre and Eddy will be there. Tie up all your personal admin and prep. Good Luck."

78

1800 hrs. Med Prep.

Eddy the Medic handed out large yellow pills, extra dressings, and green fabric pouches, one to each of them.

"Okay guys, the green packets are for real emergencies, and are not as has been suggested an inflatable life raft. They contain four standard doses of morphine. Inside the packet are four dose labels. Attach one to the casualty for each dose administered. Do not give more than two doses under any circumstances or the casualty will fall into a coma and die."

"The elephant pills are to be taken one hour before you leave; they are a very strong purgative and will give you a huge dump and clean out your bowels. It's important if you're gut shot that your bowel is empty. Next! Wash yourselves; pay particular attention to your torso and crotch areas. The cooks have heated water, and if you can, scrounge some clean clothing, especially underwear. Every step must be taken to cut down infection from wounds. Make sure your first field dressing is either taped to your webbing or helmet or carried in the pocket on your thigh. Even better carry two. Anybody wanting extra dressings, they can get them from any of the medics. Identity discs; very important if you get slotted, keep one round your neck and put the other in your boot. Any questions so far?"

"Are we carrying our own body bags up or whit?" Brian whirled on them.

"Can that gobshit for starters. We are going to do this, no problems. Everybody sticks together and we hit them like a ton of bricks while they're still shaking from the Milan detonation."

"Easy on boss, just a wee black joke."

Brian nodded.

"Seeing as its come up; casualty drills. As soon as the Milan is fired we go fast and deep into the left of the gully. Gungroup will go hard right as we clear the rise by the bunker and take the trench system under fire. Rifle group plus me will grenade the bunker and clear it out. If the fifties are still operable we'll turn them against the trenches and support the company attack with flanking fire. We inform Munro and hold until the company assault goes in and takes the pressure off us. You stop for no-one. The attack must be maintained and pushed home. If your mother is lying wounded, you step over her and carry on. If she jumps up out of the Argie trenches, you kill her. Once we hold the position every man will make sure the enemy are dead. So as there are no misunderstandings, I'll make it plain. When rifle group has cleared through you'll put one in the head of every dago in sight. Once we're secure young Robert here will chase up the gun with the ammo load, followed by Eddy to deal with anybody who is down. Tamper, I want you to carry the radio and you are close right behind me all the way. If the main attack goes pearshaped we'll push forward off the position and go hard. Top up your ammo from enemy stocks if you have to, it's the same kit as ours. There are no questions, are there?"

Private Harper, onetime cook then total nutter for volunteering for this, stuck up his hand and asked, "Why do we go forward, not back?"

"It's safer; trust me. These guys are sharp and will begin to shell the approach routes to prevent reinforcement, and once they are sure the bunker is overrun they'll plaster the whole position." Brian stood and spread the TAC map on a rock.

"The Padre will soon be up for those who want to bet all the odds. Until then, I want you to study this while the light holds and get the site fixed hard in your minds. One more thing, get hold of a whetstone. I want your bayonets sharpened."

1900 hrs.

Tamper nudged him. "Aye! Aye! Here's the sky pilot come to see us off."

Father McNeil, known to all and sundry as, 'Christ on a bike,' because of the old mountain bike he rode all round the Devon countryside, ferreting out his press ganged flock from under gorse bushes, muddy ditches, and not a few West Country police stations. He was Barra born and bred with the breadth of a fishing boat. His gigantic fisherman's hands clutched a case of Mars bars under his arm. His clothes were as filthy and reeking as the rest of them. Over his stinking combats he wore a ragged Barbour jacket which rustled at night and surprised not a few nervous sentries. An ancient steel framed rucksack and an angler's wading pole completed his battle dress. His huge cheery grin widened the nearer he came to their bivvy, where he drove his pole into the peat by the fire and dropped his kit at their feet. They all stood up.

"Hi! Padre, is that no bibles you should be carrying?"

"Maybe Brian, maybe, but they don't taste as good as Mars bars. How're you all doin' then?" He pulled an impressive 'K' bar knife from his green wellies, hunkered down and deftly

80

slit open the box, taking them all into his smile. They grinned madly back at this vision of the church militant.

"Jesus God Padre! That's some knife; I thought you were non-combatant."

"True my son, true, but I may be required to smite the ungodly."

Lured by the Mars bars the bears gathered and having trapped them Father Mac reached into his jacket and drew out a stole and communion set from an inner pocket.

"Assuming you boys have refreshed the body I have come to see to what is left of your Taurag souls, even the Sassenachs in the company."

From his ruck, he took some battered and torn prayer books wrapped in plastic followed by a bottle of Black Label, enlarging his smile till Brian thought he might swallow his ears. "The flesh is willing no doubt boys, but the spirit is 100 proof."

They huddled like small lost boys camping, under two ponchos tethered to the bank by bungees, faces highlighted by the weak torch, their stubble and dirt cast gaunt shadows. Their boots touched the sizzling Dixie in the centre and steamed off in the heat. Brian suddenly remembered an old picture of Capt. Scott's doomed men. They produced dirty mugs and Father Mac poured the whisky round till the bottle was empty and they all sat grinning inanely at each other. Outside the artillery and mortars thumped away at the Argie positions.

"We'll keep the bottle for later; we can pee in it and not leave the shelter."

"Hell's teeth Padre, Ah'll never fit ma willy intae that wee neck."

"Nor me son, but I couldnae lay ma hand on a bin at this late hour."

They had a collective cackle and fell silent, savouring being out of the wind, with whisky to drink and the warmth of being unwilling to be anywhere else or in other company at this moment.

"We should toast something," Brian suggested.

"Okay boss, on you go, fill your boots."

He thought of, 'Bloody war, sudden death and quick promotion,' but caught Harpers fearful eyes boring into his and changed mid-breath. "Home, Robert's curry house free meals. Nobody dies."

"Home, free meals," they echoed softly, "nobody dies."

Father Mac drew a waterproof folder from his old torn ruck and opening it handed each of them a pencil.

"High tech stuff for you lot, pencils with rubbers on the end. I've brought you boys up these will forms; you have to fill them out for Brigade staff."

Jones promptly used his to boost the flame under the hexi burner. "Bugger that, I've nought to leave but a huge porn collection and nobody to leave it to."

Tamper bunged his in too. "The gits! If I'm deid then, I'll no be caring who blags ma stuff."

Tonka stowed his into a pocket. "Fuck the pencilnecks Father, but I've just swallowed Eddy's huge yella pill and I'm short on bog paper."

The rest took a form and amid a communal squirming and flashing of hooded torches began to fill them in.

Brian said "Look, you can tick a box for either 'burial or cremation' or 'other disposal of remains.'"

Everyone laughed.

"In the Great War the joke had been to ask if the Army made you pay for the blanket they buried you in. Do you reckon the Mod deduct the cost of the body bag from our insurance?"

"Young Robert here can have me ashes as spice for his curry," said Fraser, "then I can give you all the shits."

"You do that already," Brian told him.

He clipped the torch to his helmet band and read the form through. Was it boredom, or was he just caught up in the system, just as much as a condemned prisoner. The prisoner who orders his last meal, then meets his family for the final time, has a last medical to see if he's fit enough to die and a last prayer meeting and finally he fills in a not dissimilar form, all in a fug of indifference at his insignificance.

Mostly they sat in companionable silence, passing the nutty and the fags, eking out the whisky, breathing deeply of its smell of far of peaty lost places. The wills were returned one by one, crumpled, slightly damp, pierced by the pencils in places; tiny bullet holes. Mac handed out letter forms and cleared his throat.

"More importantly, I'll take any letter you might want to write and have me keep for you. I'll also mail any normal letter via the censor. If you lads want to leave me a, 'just in case', private letter, don't be embarrassed. I can tell you as a priest, nobody, not even me, will ever know what it contains, and I will deliver it myself."

"Some of you may think you have nobody to write such a letter to; someone who might care or grieve for you. However, in my experience everyone has someone who is close and loves and worries about each one of us. The letters are important because, no matter what happens to each of you, or what you are compelled to do, each of you will hazard your soul tonight."

A long tearing burst of MG fire tore the fabric of the moment, a pause, and then another.

Robert started, Jonesy gulped down the last of his whisky, Fraser hunched and covered his ears.

"Whassat?" mumbled Robert.

"Sustained fire gimpeys from across the valley; they're zeroing in for the shoot. Time's getting on." Brian told him.

"Exactly my point boys," said Father Mac, placing his stole around his neck and taking of his helmet. "I know not all you boys are Catholic, some of you are nothing much in the way of religion at all, but I'm going to move off a little way to that wee outcrop over there. If anyone wants to talk or quiet their spirit, then come see me. Write your thoughts for your loved ones and bring them down to me."

He downed the last of his whisky and slapped a few helmets by way of, 'cheerio.'

"I'll see you all later in any case, for I'll come up to the assault position and will be going up behind you with Eddy and his grave robbers. So! don't be shy, no pressure."

Tamper stretched and sighed. "Man!, whisky, Mars bars, fags, shelter, warm fug, bog paper, hot water for washing, and the blessings of the collective Almighty." He grinned up at them.

"Are we fucking spoilt or whit?"

2000 hrs

For the next hour the Padre crouched in the lee of the boulder. All of them except Fraser and Brian made their way down to him. Brian squatted over a discarded Argie helmet, his trousers around his ankles, washing himself in the two inches of water it contained. When he was dried he would put on the last of his clean pants and a stinking but only slightly grubby 'T' shirt, the best he could manage.

Surprise! Surprise! the promised bath of hot water had not materialised. The medics handed out handfuls of alcohol wipes and they set to. In the fading light, he could see Father

Mac and Robert kneeling by the rocks, helmeted heads touching, Mac's hand falling on the boy's shoulder then moving in that ageless sign of benediction and cleansing of the spirit. When the boy came back up, he looked sheepishly at Brian then lowered his eyes.

"Well," he said, "you never know, just backing all my horses."

"Don't apologise to anyone here, son. I might even go down myself. George Patton said there were no atheists in foxholes. Everybody screaming for either Christ or their mother."

"Will it be bad, Sgt?" he whispered.

"It'll be dark and bloody, flashes, bangs, explosions, shouting, screaming, and things in the air. Focus on the job in hand, do as Fraser says and you'll be just fine."

2045 hrs.

Brian took one final drag at his smoke, slowly ground it out against the rock and stood up. The rest of them detected the movement and turned towards his shadow shape. The night was clear as crystal and the southern sky whirled above them filled with countless stars. Was it Kipling who wrote a poem on that? He couldn't remember. If he'd paid more attention at school he wouldn't be bloody here now, would he? The hollow bang of the harassing fire came every few moments, the muzzle flashes highlighting the crews, as stark as x-rays against the side of the cut

The bears watched silently, as he pulled on his helmet, their faces closed; all of them struck dumb. There was no return fire from up the hill, but they knew what was coming and would conceal their positions until the last moment.

Brian had a sudden and aching physical need to hold his wee girl. To awake from this and walk her to school. For an instant, he felt her in his arms and he could smell her Barbie shampoo and talc. Emotion had ambushed him and unwarranted, a small sound leaked from his throat, before he turned towards the bears.

"Okay boys."

He checked the time and snapped the cover back over.

"Saddle up! Cpl! Get the men moving, by this rock in ten minutes."

Father Mac loomed at his side. "What about you Brian, is there nothing I can do for you, do you have a letter for the

84

family?"

"Tried to write Father, but just dried up, too focused on the job in hand, too tired out. Nothing comes. Any suggestions?"

Father Mac nodded. "It's hard to say what you want without sounding false. You have to reach into yourself, find what you want to say and tell her simply and honestly, what you feel. In my experience women know what's true and what's not."

Brian grinned at him in the fading light. "Father! You old scunner, what experience. Is this confession time for you as well?"

The priest laughed loudly, shattering the quiet and turning nervous glances their way.

"Ah! well now, you see I was a late vocation. Before that, I was in the RN for seven years. Seen it, done it, caught and cured it, got the 'T' shirt."

He took Brian's arm, drew him to the side and hunkered down. "Speaking of confession Brian, I know you're a Catholic, will you not take the sacrament before you all go up the gully and maybe get yourselves plastered?"

Brian took off his helmet and the woolly hat under it. The cold wind took his matted hair and lifted it freezing the bugs in his scalp into stillness.

"I'd feel like a cheat at the last minute Father, you know? Trying to scrape in at the last minute after not giving a toss since I was sixteen. If I went into a Chapel the bloody roof would come in. Besides, it would take too long."

Father Mac's arm went around his shoulder.

"You could just stick to the highlights, mortal sins, juicy stuff; leave the general dross of general badness. What would you say it you did confess?"

Brian said nothing. He gazed across the shoulder of the hill where the gully was. Tracer lofted silently in a lazy arc into the dark maw of the gully. Lines of light, the road to eternity well lit and signposted. What if it all went tot shit? What if there was something after this? What if this was, 'it' after years of not being sure. Mum used to say, once a Catholic always a Catholic. They always got you in the end.'

A figure came over from the huddle by the boulder. He knew it was Tamper, the box shape of the Clansman radio large on his back, the whip aerial marking him down for the snipers.

"Two section is all closed up and ready for sea boss. The set is netted in and Munro says start time is delayed for twenty minutes. There's been a 'blue on blue' in front of 'M' company, total fucking chaos. All units are to hold at present locations."

"Total Snafu! Right! Pass the word to the boys and tell them to rest for now."

"Roger Boss." Tamper scampered away. Brian turned back to Father Mac.

"I'd tell her I was sorry for cheating on her in Belize. And Norway, and fucking Bosnia. Sorry for the rows and the tempers. For never bloody being there. For all the times I've hurt her and left her alone. The swearing, the drinking, the times I lost it and shouted at her and the wee one."

"I'm sorry for shooting that Argie boy at Acacia House. He just popped up in front of me and I was tensed up on full automatic. He had his hands up, no weapon, even adrenalised to the eyeballs I could see that. Just didn't register, double tapped him and rolled clear. Like when you're slamming the car door to lock it and the keys are still in the ignition, you know? Your brain shouts no but your hand closes the door anyway. I felt bad about that. I felt worse later because it didn't bother me at the time."

Brian stopped. It had all poured out of him after all, burst dam syndrome, he smiled and laughed.

"Ma Mammy, she'd be awful pleased."

Father Mac nodded. "Aye, right enough. Mothers know best."

He helped Brian lift his equipment and throw it on, holding his Sterling smg for him while he fastened everything. When Brian tried to take it, Father Mac held it and checked him, moving his face close to Brian's he whispered softly in his ear.

"Ego te absolve peccatis tuis, in nominee Patri, et Fillii, et Spiritu Sancto, Amen. Go in peace and sin no more."

Brian tugged the weapon away.

"Fat fucking chance of sin here. You sneaky bastard Father."

Father Mac shook his hand firmly. "That I am Brian, that I am. Good luck now, I'll see you on the start line."

2200 hrs.

Total black and not your city dark, with its streetlamps and car lights. Primeval dark. Where all you know is that your feet are on the ground and you're facing uphill. Not that Brian could take his eyes off the glowing compass dial clutched in his hand. It was just over one 'K' to the start line, marked by a razor ridge in line with Longden and the south peak. He'd established that was about 1500 paces on the flat which would be about 1700 to compensate for the uphill leg. Munro would be up there with the Milan team and engineers. There would be a blue light towards him which he should see soon. That's if he wasn't bloody lost, an idea Fraser grew more vocal with as time passed.

He stopped to consult with Jonesy who was pace counting, leaning close, helmets touching.

"What do you have?"

"I think we've overshot, missed it. I make it 1645 paces at the moment yet we're still going downhill. I think we're too far south, I think we should veer uphill."

Brian took the humph. "I think the dwarves had longer legs than you. I'm thinking you couldn't find your arse in the dark with both hands. Take five! Fraser! Put the gimpy uphill twenty metres." He shrugged out of his gear.

"Tonka and I will recce forward on 900 mils bearing and return same way. Anybody comes at you from any other direction; kill them!" Tonka materialised beside him, the remainder of the section facing alternate direction to give all round fire and settled down to wait. Brian quickly briefed him.

"I'm off track a bit, so we'll recce forward about 500 metres; any questions?"

"Why fucking me? Ah'm happy you've given me this opportunity to shine in adversity, Sgt."

"Shuttit! Return bearing is 4100 mils, stay on my rear and watch your step. Ready?"

"Oh aye, jist gaggin' tae get on."

They checked their weapons, one in the breech, safety on, and slid away up the hill. The dark was filled with sounds. The harsh overture of the battle winding up surrounded them in the night. The heavy thump of the artillery rounds being walked onto targets for a battery shoot. Heavy machine gun and mortar fire being zeroed in by spotter. Desultory fire from lesser weapons as patrols out in the void demonstrated to cover assault engineers lifting and marking routes. It was not these they strained for, these would not kill them; yet. The small noises would kill them now. The missed footfall, the ignored crunch of gravel, the rub of cloth on webbing, grass brushing over combat clothing, the soft snick of a safety catch. Manmade metallic sounds; loose rounds in a pouch, belted ammo unsecured; a cough, a sneeze, hissed words of warning. That final sound a grenade makes as the detonator clicks a millisecond before it shreds you to bloody pulp. And all this could pass unnoticed because the wind is in your ear.

Brian stopped and checked his course. Truth was, he had to stop; he was trembling, clothes and body slick with sweat, what they politely called, 'emotional sweating.' My arse! It was a total funk, it was lashing off him 'cos he was shitting it. Every blade of grass, every time he put his foot down, every whisper in the wind was winding him up tighter and tighter. The sweat had screwed up his peripheral vision. He tugged out his scrim neckie and wiped his face, smearing the cam cream and tugging the stubble painfully.

Tonka seemed calm in the extreme, hunkered quietly, head turning to watch the shadows, waiting for orders. Perfect soldier. Tonka tensed against Brian and froze, slowly sliding his rifle barrel over Brian's left shoulder and pointing it uphill to a dim telltale of dull blue light. Brian nodded and showed Tonka a fist then pointed to the ground, translated as, bring the section here.

Alone in the dark he began to shiver and froze. Christ! He had been lost, might have got them all ambushed and killed. He vomited between his knees, rank bitter bile mixed with the remains of Tampers sludge food meal. Just tired was all, tired and cold and fed up. Who was he kidding? He was afraid and not up to it. The Bears arrived as he vomited again and waited stolidly for him to finish. Nobody said anything. Jonesy passed him his gear and said, "bearing is 870 mils."

2300 hrs.

"You're adrift." Munro hissed, his helmet touching Brian's.

"Me and the whole fucking battle by all accounts. We got lost, sue me. What happened down at the company position, we heard a lot of firing?"

"Blue on blue. The engineers lifting your mines drifted off course on the way in and got bumped by a returning patrol from recce troop who shot them up. 'B' company thought their patrol was being ambushed and opened up with everything they had at short range. Triggered their claymores."

88

"What's the score?"

"Five dead, six wounded, two very serious. Davie Sheridan was Oic."

"What a plonker."

"He's a dead plonker now, which will make you Colour Sgt; after this."

Munro checked his watch.

"All units are to hold on present locations, new start time is 0005, this is your Milan team."

Two scarecrow figures lurked against the rock face amid a rubbish heap of gear. "Good luck, see you on the top." They shook hands and Munro slunk off down the hill with his radio op.

Brian informed the section, got the usual reaction. "Couldn't organise an orgy in a brothel."

They quieted when he informed them of the blue on blue casualties and they thought how easy it could happen to them, even if they were careful.

"Jonesy!" he hissed. "Put out two claymores twenty metres uphill on either flank and set up the gimpy to cover the slope. Section orders in ten minutes, in the meantime get an ammo and kit check done."

He had to write, he had to write now. It overwhelmed him, the need to say something, leave a word or two, just in case. Things damned up burst into words in his head. He dumped his gear and pulled the poncho over his head to cover the torch. Cocooned there safe in the womb of the red torch light and very aware of how little time he had, the pencil sped across the page. Everything hidden and unexpressed pouring out to his wife and daughter. He wrote with a ferocious instinct, until Jones tapped him on the helmet and he signed quickly, then folded the letter card into a poly bag.

2310 hrs.

Mad Alec and his sidekick Ross were waiting. Their skill with the missile was legendary. They had taken down a chopper at San Carlos, stood up in the open under fire and chopped it out of the sky. Ross was nicknamed, 'Marty', for his huge staring eyes which regarded Brian unblinkingly. Twin headlights in the cammed out face. Brian noticed they had two missiles after all.

"Are you set up?"

"Aye!"

"I thought they were only deploying one missile."

"What the fuck do they know; pencilneck bastards? I need the tools for the job and it wis lying there gaggin tae be fired."

"Do you have a plan?"

"Aye."

Jesus Christ!, this was like pulling teeth. Brian held his temper and waited a count of ten. These two were fucking mad, they liked it here.

"Do you think you might tell me what it is?"

Alec leaned forward the better to see him, blew his nose in his hand and wiped it in the grass.

"Me and ma mucker have crawled up the gully a wee way, and in the middle about twenty metres below the crest is this huge rock. It's a blind spot, 'tween us and the bunker slit. We slide up there when you say wi' the two tubes, and when we're ready we slot wan right in the front windae. The second tube we'll fire straight down the support trench and gie them a wee fright."

"Do you have a fallback plan, in case you miss?"

Ross snorted and spat, raising his eyebrows in contempt, insulted into speech.

"See us china, we don't fucking miss. Deid bastards miss."

Jones tugged at his sleeve. "Father Mac is here and so is Eddy and his grave robbers."

Brian nodded at Alec and Ross then withdrew from their lunatic presence.

Fraser checked his weapon again and sat staring blindly uphill to where he knew the bunker was. He had a very bad feeling about this, he had to get out of here. He began to think of the disowned son he had by that lassie in Liverpool, who'd be five now. The reason he was here was because he'd fled all responsibility and never looked back. That had been a bad thing. Now his demons whispered *'You're going to die, you're going to die,'* with absolute certainty. He screwed his eyes tight shut muttering into the grass, "we're all going to get fucking killed."

The gimpy rested on its bipod beside him, he couldn't stop his shaking hand snicking the safety catch on and off, a metronome of building panic. Soapy Souter's hand grabbed his.

"Goannie stoap that?" he hissed. "What the Hell's up wi'

you? You're doin' ma brain in."

Final Orders.

"Okay! Is everybody here?" Brian scanned the indistinct figures crouched by the crag. "If you're no here pit yer haun up."

Some grins, a few feeble cracks.

"Ah'm kidding on Ah'm no here, does that count?" The Milan team came slithering out of the murk.

"Thought we'd come and see what you lot had in mind, just in case you got us kilt." Alec growled.

"Where's your kit?" Brian demanded.

"Up at the final pos just below the boulder; it'll save us humping back and forth."

"Aye!, Right! Save us humping it up and doon like bloody yo-yo's" Ross confirmed.

Brian opened his mouth then shut it. He could sit here for hours arguing the toss with Alec and his moronic sidekick. He gave in and nodded; had to trust them.

"Okay, the bunker is sixty metres from our jump off, bearing 190 magnetic; phase one will be the Milan team, Alec?"

"Listen up; me and Ross have reccied the gap while you lot were wandering about lost. Fifty metres short of the bunker is a huge fucking rock that the stupid Dagoes have left in their line of sight. Ross and me will be in position with both tubes ten minutes before time. We'll slot one through their slit right on time, so don't be late ladies, then move right and give the other one to the fifty cal in the trench system. Then we bug out for coffee and Mars bars."

"Fucking right, Tora Peachy!" said Ross.

Brian nodded. "Phase two. When the Milan team move the assault group will move up in single file and take cover under the big flake of rock to the left of the gully, Gungroup will move slightly right of that for protecting fire. Immediately the first Milan is fired the assault section will go forward. Soapy and CJ, concentrate on the slit, Pudsey with Tonka move left and grenade the entry. Rapid fire, follow up quickly and make sure you finish everyone who is down, two in the head as you pass. Fraser will open up sustained fire on the trench system and stop any reinforcement of the bunker. Tamper, you're with me, stay close with the radio. Young Harper, stay close up with Jonesy, five or six metres behind and keep your head down. When he shouts for ammo up you come like hell."

What next?, He sweated a moment while his thoughts ran clear of fire and then he nodded.

"Eddy, you don't move till the bunker is silenced, then come on up and deal with anybody down along our axis. Father Mac, you can be anywhere you like. Fight right through till we overlook the trenches, put a grenade into each one. Gungroup will then come up and lay suppressing fire onto any threat. Tamper and I will reinforce at any point as required and once we all close up, he and I will clear the bunker. Tamper will put two white phos through the slit, then two frags; I will do clearance. Re-org on the sheltered side then move left and lay down fire on the positions to the west. Break up any move to counterattack with max firepower. Use any operable Argie stuff. Remember to check and shift fire as 'M' company attack passes across our front. Do not wander all over the gully, stay to the left on the approach until the Milan team fires. All going well it should be all over in fifteen."

He didn't ask for questions, no point. He looked at each one

"Right! Stand up!"

Brian took Father Mac by the sleeve and pressed the letter cards in to his hand.

"Hold this lot for me till I get back down," then he turned quickly away before Father Mac could say anything.

Standing in front of the section he surveyed them one by one. He wouldn't allow his sister out with any one of them, or trust them with a girl over sixteen. Hell! He wouldn't leave them alone with a ladies laundry basket or a well dressed female corpse, but he would go up the gully with them.

Pep talk time, final jokes, last reminders.

"Heads up! We can do this boys. Don't stop. Be fast. Be hard. Be quick. Remember your drills, let your buddy know when you reload, and when you throw grenades. Remember you're throwing uphill, so it could roll back unless you place it right. Keep grenades where you can reach them and follow the explosion as close as you can. Fire on the move, maximum disruption. Check your fire, count your rounds, positive id on targets outside the bunker complex. Watch your angles."

They stared back at him, Jones and Tamper smiling, it was time to stop gabbling. Passing down the line, he made the final checks on them, pulling and tugging at straps and loose gear. As he came to each one he made eye contact under the

92

dark helmet brims and had them jump up and down listening for rattles. Satisfied, he stepped back.

"Okay! Milan team, Alec! Move out."

He pulled a double magazine from his pouch, one taped to the other for speed. "Load!"

Soft rustlings, muted metallic snicks as the mags locked into housings. Soft sounds of Death. Fraser loaded the gimpy with a belt of fifty, laying it across his forearm and shoulder. Young Robert grunted and hefted the four ammo liners, a belt of two hundred loose in coils around his neck. The latest in martial jewellery.

"Ready!"

They pulled the cocking levers smoothly and silently to the rear chambering a round, safety catches snicked on.

"Fix bayonets."

A soft hiss as the air rushed into the scabbard, metallic fumbling and the click as the ring thudded into place over the barrel and locked in the bayonet lug. Something terminal about that. All the jokes and bullshit and stalling over; nobody had anything funny to say, as their brains numbed with the implications and dreadful finality. They all stared mesmerised at their blade, unable to drag their eyes off it.

Robert raised a hesitant hand. "Mines, are they all lifted, what if we run into mines on the way in, what do I do?"

"If you find a mine," Tamper told him, "You'll be the most unconcerned bastard in the gully. You'll be too busy screaming and trying to count your legs and balls. Got it?"

Brian held up his hand for quiet. "If we hit mines when we go in you'll just have to keep going."

He pointed uphill and kept it all simple.

"You're on your feet, you have all your gear and you're mostly awake. So, that way, turn. Move in single file behind me, no sound from here on in, not even if the man behind you stabs you in the arse. Follow me!"

Would they? Would they follow him he wondered? Every commander's nightmare since the Roman army. What would he do if they all just lay there and he looked back to find he was on his own?

Did they respect him enough to follow him up the gully. Once they were on the move they would be compelled to carry on through. The first move was the crisis, not what followed.

What made a man move his arms and legs, lift his body

93

up into a storm of steel when every instinct shrieked at him to dig a hole a hundred foot deep and stay in it?

He would soon know, one way or the other. Acacia House had been different, a company attack almost like a scheme on Dartmoor, they had been virgins then. Now he was in command, and began to suffer the erosive doubts and isolation of every leader since Christ rode a donkey.

2330 hrs

Despite the cold, sweat was slick on their skins when moving, freezing on their flesh when they halted, chilling their hearts. Keeping direction was not as bad as expected, when Brian lifted his head he could make out the dark outline of the shoulder below the bunker. Their boots skidded and ground on the loose rock underfoot. He prayed nobody would dislodge a boulder and send it crashing down. He could read the battle by its noises. Heavy Troop had begun to drop seemingly random mortar round around the south shoulder, but creeping it towards the impact points for the assault.

For now, they kept the enemies' heads down and in their slits, harassing the trenches and stopping movement. Machine gun fire from across the valley increased, the tracers going over their head and giving them direction on the objective. Golden fingers of light, broken by red and green; five invisible rounds between them. The Argies got nervous and began to interdict the approaches to their positions all along the slope, but Two Section were already under the guns. Sooner them than us, was the thought of every soul there. Small nervous firefights broke out down to their left as jittery OP's on both sides put out defensive fire.

A flare went up from the Argie support trenches to their left, hissing all the way up in a terrible sparkling curve. They fell face down into the tall grass and scrub, until it burst into blinding brilliance and began to swing down on its parachute. Even with his eyes screwed shut Brian could still see the light. They must see us. Now we get it and he waited, helpless, for the warning shout then the shredding stammer of the fifty cal. Slowly the flare fell to earth behind them, while they played a deadly version of boyhood statues. Brian's nose brushed the gravel, the grass poked his eyes and stuffed inside his helmet. He could see an ant peering at him, the pyrites in the small rocks glinting like tiny jewels. This ant was going to outlive him. The rocks would endure long after he was gone.

The flare died and left them in a pit dark as tar. What a stupid recruit mistake, opening his eyes, he was blind. He pulled his compass and made out he was checking the bearing then flowed to his feet, kicked Jones, and began the slithering crouch up towards the flake of rock which he could now see. He hoped the Argies were blinded as well.

Alec and Ross were so well cammed out he tramped on them before a hand tugged at his trousers. He slid down beside them while the rest of the section bumped to a halt behind him and faded into the grass under cover of the flake. They were all huffing and puffing like a bloody train, faces slick, their cam cream running. How could the Argies not hear them? Ross and Alec were ready. They had unpacked the tubes and, disregarding every safety procedure had armed them and switched on.

Alec held his watch under Brian's nose, indicated his direction and the team slithered away to the firing point making no more noise than the wind in the grass.

Brian put his helmet next to Jones and whispered, "ten minutes." Jones passed it down the line and when he tapped Brian on the leg and gave him a nod. They moved out, crawling now, trying to muffle every sound, senses acute, nerves screaming at every pebble turning under their bodies. Pausing at every rub of webbing as they squeezed through the angle formed by the fallen rock. Bang! Clank! Freeze!

Stop breathing, stop thinking, stop making plans for anything. Pucker up, adrenaline is brown. Harper! Harper you useless fuck, dragging an ammo liner over a rock. They lay for a year like a paralysed snake. Brian wanted to stay here behind this strong eternal rock forever. Nothing happened. He swallowed, drew breath, felt bile in his throat and relaxed so much he pissed himself.

At the assault position he turned to Jones, held up a clenched fist, pointed to the ground. Fraser and Harper appeared with the gimpy, Brian pointed out a slight hollow to his left just below the crest where they could take both the slit and the left flank under the arc of the gun. They nodded and crept past him. Brian checked the time and whispered in Tamper's ear. "One minute, pass it back."

They waited, pressed together in the small dip, each silent now in their own lonely place. Brian's skin felt dull, his limbs heavy and unresponsive, fingers numb, eyes watering, his crotch burning with urine. He put his head down, keep me safe for my little girl.

Jones gripped the night glasses, ready for when the dance started to kneel up and direct fire on priority targets. His whole body trembled, just cold, just cold.

Fraser crushed the butt of the gimpy into his shoulder and tried to control his ragged breathing, the dull rounds on the belt curling over his left hand, clear of the grass. A voice in his head dinned repeatedly at him. "You're fucked son, fucked!; remember your stoppage drills, short bursts, don't twist the belt; you're fucking dead, son."

Robert hid behind a boulder, the belt of two hundred draped around his neck twice, the points digging into the flesh. He could feel blood. His fingers clutched at the handles of two liners, one in each hand and each hand beyond the point of numbness. His rifle dug into his back. Filled with terror, he was unaware that he was silently weeping.

Pudsey, CJ, Tonka and Soapy lay on their sides, backs pressed against the rock, knees drawn up in readiness to push off. Eyes glazed, their breathing grew faster as they hyperventilated. They all pushed off their safety catches and began to lift themselves onto their elbows. Their brains ran at Mach 2 over checks.

WP in right pouch, spare frags in left, ready mags in breast pockets, field dressing on webbing, morphine under helmet liner. Move fast. Move hard. Kill everybody you meet. Don't stop. Final RV at left of bunker. What the fuck am I doing here?

In the bunker above them Private third class Ernesto Jones, a barber from Cello Ponte, was being soundly thumped by his Sgt for betraying the position without orders, but insisted he had fired the flare because he had definitely seen something in the gully. The Sgt peered through the slit, his night vision gone, the dark filled with blurs of red and green across his vision. The British fire had certainly increased. What was that, there, by the rock in the middle of the gully? Was it a sheep?

All the mortar fire began to concentrate and it became impossible to speak. The tracer over their heads was solid as all the guns joined in. The Sgt fired another flare, this time down the gully. It soared high and exploded behind them. When it ignited, Brian knew it would silhouette them. The area to their front exploded with fire as the mortars plastered the approaches, prior to lifting off and boxing the objective. Shrapnel, and clumps of earth carried by the blast shot over their heads or pattered on their backs. Totally nervous now, the Argies began to fire on fixed lines.

The air was filled and crashed with thunderous noise, beating at their ears. The ground pounded and rippled beneath them. Shards of rock and debris rained on them, as all cowered in position aware only of the small area in which they lay. Brian forced himself to his knees and peered over the curve of the rise to orientate the axis of attack.

Out in the gully the Milan team came into action and Alec rose to his feet and shouldered the launcher.

Brian screamed at them, "Go! Go! Go!" and pumped his fist up and down as the flare ignited.

Somebody got hit in the Argie trench and he shrieked, shrill with despair.

Mad Alec dropped to one knee to throw off the Argie gunners aim, searching for him in the dark and put the dot on the slit. Ross sat up, removed the flash cover and skelped him on the top of the helmet before dropping down to ready the second tube. Alec fired; the Milan ignited throwing a jet of flame to the rear, hesitated, then streaked away.

Almost immediately the Argie gunner found the range and Alec's head disappeared in a cloud of blood and bone; his body standing erect for a second more, before crumpling, with the launcher still clasped in his twitching hands.

On cue, Fraser slid the gun over the two rocks to his front and opened fire on the bunker slit, raking the fire across until the tracer became swallowed in the slit, as it searched out the occupants. Robert, totally unnerved by the battle, huddled gibbering and deaf behind a rock, digging holes with his feet and elbows.

CJ and Pudsey stood up and flung two grenades, one WP, one smoke in front of the bunker. Tonka moved left and standing in a small niche let loose a handheld Laws rocket down the support trench.

The Milan shot forward, struck the top of the rise and slammed into the base of the bunker detonating in a thunderous glare and white hot flash.

The assault squad ran into the blast which staggered them, inflicting them with slight unnoticed wounds, then they resumed their crouching stilted run, all spreading out and firing from the hip. Jones detected movement from the support trench to the left and directed Fraser onto the target. Shrieks and screaming came from there, from men cut to pieces only ten metres from the muzzle of the gun. Fraser was screaming dementedly at the top of his voice. "Ammo! Ammo! Ammo up!"

Somebody else operated Robert's body and pushed him up the gully to the gun, gasping and shouting incoherently, blind to everything except the muzzle flash of the gun and that he had to get there.

He fell beside Fraser, now down to twenty on the belt and feverishly attached the long belt to the flapping wriggling end. His lost fingernail went unnoticed in the racing breech.

Only one fifty was firing, high at first but now correcting down onto them. Once the gunner got the range, the other would join in. Brian had to get them moving; he tossed another grenade then rose up shouting, "Follow me!", and pounded up the rise in slow motion firing from the hip. The smoke was thick and he raced into its blanket, his path lit by the storm of fire, the crash and crack of frags and the steady thump of the traversing fifty cal. They all followed him.

CJ overtook him, crouching down and firing into the bunker entrance. Just as Brian came up someone popped up and put two rounds into CJ's side and he collapsed without a sound. Emptying his rifle into the bunker, Brian dropped into the trench. A blurred shadow fumbling for a magazine confronted him, and carried on by his momentum Brian thrust his bayonet into the man's chest. He heard bone break and the gristle thump as the blade went fully home with his falling weight behind it. The man gasped in shock then expelled an explosive sound like a burst tyre.

Brian was shrieking insanely now pressing fully home forcing the figure to the ground, aware of nothing but the writhing man staring at him in frog-eyed shock, and with both of his hands clasped around the rifle muzzle, pleading with his eyes and whimpering in Spanish. Brian tried to pull the blade free, by twisting and grinding the blade, but the writhing Argie, with blood pouring from his mouth and his heels drumming on the floor of the trench, held on like grim death. Brian screamed at him to let go then fired twice. The blade was blasted free and Brian stabbed three or four times, before collapsing against the sandbags, with his chest heaving, his brain reeling and his soul dying.

The other fifty men were still in action, searching for Fraser's muzzle flashes and rounds as big as thumbs punched through the earth bank. Jones ran across and grabbed hold of Fraser's gear harness.

"Move! Move you bastard. He'll kill you in a minute. Move with me."

The instant Jones and Fraser came to their feet the fifty traversed onto them, clods of earth, rock, and ricochets sparked and clattered all around them.

They would never make the side of the bunker, Fraser realised, not like this, caught out here in the open. The angles were all wrong. He lost it then. Hefting the gimpy under his arm, he charged the slit, with his gun flaming and he screeched and gibbered like a harpy from Hell. Jones followed him on instinct; sobbing and screaming "Awe Shit! Awe Shit" over and over again, as he rolled a frag underarm which bounced across the ten metres and plopped into the slit.

"Grenade!" he screamed and dropped down trying to fit his whole body inside his helmet.

Fraser kept going, the gimpy spitting it's fire non-stop into the slit and flopped down on his knees before it, shoving the still firing gun inside the bunker, raking it from side to side, searching for targets, wreaking havoc inside. His demented gibbering was only halted by the dull thump of the grenade, followed by the sympathetic detonation of munitions in the bunker. The flash enveloped him, shrapnel tore at his throat and eyes piercing his chest and shredding both thighs. The belt ran out with a musical tinkle and the steaming barrel fell silent.

Jones dashed up and tried to lift him clear, but his kneeling body was held in position by the gun, posing like a bloody supplicant from Hell.

Jones screamed "Ammo up! Ammo up!"

Robert came; gasping rattling and stumbling, falling beside them his eyes rolling as he tried to squeeze his whole body into the slight dip in front of the slit, his heels kicking in the gorse and his fingers scrabbling for Fraser's morphine and dressing.

Jones shoved Harper away and pulled Fraser over on his back and away from the gun. He checked the action and changed the barrel, then reloaded a new liner.

"He's hit; Jesus fucking Christ! Help him!"

He darted a glance at Robert. "Lets get a fucking grip!

99

Here! Promotion in the field, you're now the gunner."

He grabbed Robert's harness and dragging him tore over to the group of rocks to the left.

"Counterattack any minute, get fire down on the approach trenches, Now!"

Hysterical, Robert pulled the gun into his shoulder and cocked the breech. Jones peered through his night glasses and gave his fire orders. "Half right!; at fifty metres; enemy troops in trench; FIRE!"

Screeching defiance, Robert opened fire; Jones threw the last of the frags and white phos.

In the light of the muzzle flash and explosions they could see the writhing men jerking and falling, trapped by the steep side of the trench. They could hear the blubbering of the wounded and the solid meaty slap of the rounds hitting muscle and bone.

"Reload! Who's here?" Brian roared. "Gungroup, stand fast. Remainder On me! On me!"

Figures dropped into the trench. Pudsey, Soapy, Tonka, with Tamper humping the radio and trying to drag CJ.

"Anybody hit apart from CJ? No? Right! Share out the grenades among you. Tonka. Take the liners in this bay over to the gun, they're on the left flank hitting the support elements."

Tonka nodded and took off.

"Tamper? Try and raise Munro, tell him the ducks have landed. You two, let's clear this bunker then reinforce the gun and shred the Argie flank. Grenades!"

Soapy and Pudsey pulled one frag and one white phos. And lobbed them into the entry, they all dropped to the deck. The blast in the confined space was deafening. Painfully, stray shrapnel tingled and clattered about them.

"IN! IN! IN!"

Brian dived into the pit first, followed by Pudsey with his smg, filling the interior with metal and noise. Someone was shrieking in the corner, a short burst cut that off. Soapy crouched by the entry and as the smoke cleared, began to shoot each of the downed Argi in the head.

Through the slit, Brian could see the bloody shambles that had been Fraser. He could see the gun team shooting up the counterattack and their shouts of demonic triumph.

Something tugged feebly at his leg, and stooping he found a horribly injured soldier, his arm nearly torn off and one side of his head shot and lying open. He pleaded in soft Spanish. Horrified, Brian tried to find the man's medikit. Pudsey leant over his shoulder and shot Ernesto the barber in the middle of the forehead, exploding his skull over the sandbags.

"Sod that pish boss, there's still a fucking rammy going on."

Brian puked bile until his muscles jangled. Pudsey pulled out his canteen, took a swig and passed it round.

Tamper came hurtling in and skidded on the blood slick floor, the weight of the radio taking him down. He came up covered in gore, frantically brushing at it with his hands and he freaked, losing it completely, until Soapy thumped him. Brian took hold of him and grabbed his hands.

"Stop gibbering. Did you get Munro?"

Tamper stopped wriggling and answered.

"He acknowledged. Said to hold fast and support the company as the main attack comes in. It's coming now."

The fire falling outside was staggering now and the earth jumped and trembled underfoot and then they could feel the action move towards the north, falling on the main Argentinean positions.

"Okay, reload and follow me." Brian plunged out and ran towards the outcrop where Robert and Jones were still pouring fire onto the Argie flank.

In the gully, Fast Eddy found Alec, took one look and stepped over him. One of the medics labelled him and left Ross cradling the shattered head. The two medics were knick-named Stackem and Bagem.

They next came upon Fraser, kneeling in the maw of the bunker with his head and his arms thrown back. His torso and thighs were in bloody rags and his eyes and mouth gaped in an expression of amazement in what was left of his face.

Father Mac would see to him. Another body, CJ's, lay at the steps down to the trench. Two rounds through and through, ribs smashed and exposed. Under his heels, the ground was gouged and his fingers were tightly clenched around his field dressing, which was jammed into his blood soaked smock. They knew he must have died here quietly and alone, while the fight went on.

They entered the reeking tomb of the bunker and began to sort through the shambles for signs of life. Eddy wondered if he had enough bags and casualty labels with him.

The rest of the section lay by the now silent gun and watched the main assault. They were out of belted link for the gun and Brian told Soapy and Pudsey to go back for one of the fifties and boxed ammo, just in case. His nose was clogged with snot and blood. Cordite and oil stank his breath, and his mouth reeked with the coppery taste of blood and mucus.

Low groans and whimpering came from the trench to their front and the air was filled with the stench of phosphorous on flesh.

Tamper punched the radio. "I can't raise anybody on this bag of shite. Can we move up to the crest?"

Brian took off his helmet and nodded, relishing the wind over his scalp, he stood with his eyes closed and thought of his girls.

"Thank you God, thank you." He whispered. "Somebody see if they can get a brew going" he told the rest and helped Tamper with the gear.

Still fucking nuthin" Tamper muttered and Brian grabbed hold of the extension and took it out into the gully. He stood on a rock and hoisted it above his head.

"Try to the right a wee bit. Get it higher," Tamper shouted.

"Bossy bastard." Brian called back. He dumped his kit and weapon, lit a fag and trailed the wire higher up the slope. On his second step, he heard a klick.

Eddy heard the crack and the thump and saw the flash through the slit. He knew exactly what it was and followed by his crew, grabbed the trauma bag and legged it towards the smoke plume and ducked their heads against the still descending debris. It had been a claymore, facing down the slope and spraying its blast and ball bearings in a razor arc downhill. Brian had a sensation of falling and landed on his right side, head down.

Very alert, he could see Tamper, splayed in a wet bloody smear over the rocks; nothing about him seemed to be shaped right. His gear and helmet were gone and he was doing a broken puppet imitation. Overhead, the stars glinted imperiously down on him, detached and cold. Queer! He could see both ways at once, that wasn't normal. He began to titter, but it hurt and he stopped. He tried to move but nothing worked. Bloody stupid; he could only flail his left arm a bit but not stop it. It had a life of its own. He looked at his hand still holding the aerial before blood ran into his eyes making him blink furiously. Eddy will be here in a jiffy, sort this out, he thought. How bad can it be?

Eddy skidded to a halt beside him and sank down to his knees. "Brian, Brian, hold on pal, you'll be dancing in no time at all. Just a wee scratch, worse than it looks."

Brian grinned at him as he began to feel lethargic and drowsy. Everything okay now; be home soon. The medics swung into action, Eddy taking control and making voice notes.

"Right! We have traumatic amputation of the left leg at knee; of the right arm at shoulder; heavy blood loss and shock imminent. Right eye out and lying on cheek; multiple lesions and gashes overall. Get an IV in and give morphine standard dose for now. Get those exposed veins tidied and covered. You! Monitor breathing and pulse, treat for shock."

Brian found it all a bit of a nuisance. Just let him lie here a while and he'd be right in no time. Auch! Eddy! Don't cut off ma arctic smock, Linda bought me that. Just let me be, what were they doing, pulling and hauling at him? It was cold lying here with his clothes cut off. The lines went into his arm, blood and morphine, dressing packages torn open fluttered and blew around like confetti.

Jeez Eddy boy, that's some set of shears you have there, I could have done with them when I was laying the carpet before I came away. God! What a sky. Shining like the glitter on Catriona's party dress. So many stars. Something popped and gushed in his chest and he gasped and vomited blood. Everything stopped working. His breathing wouldn't work with his chest muscles, it all seemed disjointed and out of kilter.

Eddy flung him on his back shouting at him. "Brian, Brian, you've got to help me here."

Brian laughed in his head. "Fuck off Eddy and gie us peace. Move your head stupid and let me look at the sky, ya balloon ye." His chest spasmed and they drew his head back forcing an airway down his gullet and pumped the bag. Eddy began to pump his chest forcing blood in buckets into the bag.

His eye dangled in the grass, that was sore. This was new, he could see the earth and sky at the same time in finite detail. See coming and going as Dad would say. Funny as hell.

Then all the stars went out.

Betty McKellar

Where the Poppies Grow

I saw her on the train
a waif girl,
looked again
at the fragility of her.
She was porcelain,
hair pre-Raphaelite
flame
copper-polished
spread like rippling molten metal
over a frame
thin as a flower stem
skin pale light, white as butterfly wing.

Beauty sings
I listened,
heard her wild today music in the discord of a silent cry
the ancient sigh from a sad clarsach.
She was tomorrow's
Deirdre of the sorrows;
her eyes knew
where the black night poppies grew
opaque as opiate
grey as clouds of held-in-rain
closing on pain

She slept
knees to her chin like a child;
she was a child.

Inside my oldness
I wept.

The Glove

I spied the glove
from the balcony above.
It was directly below
lying on empty space
long and thin
a slim hand
serene in an elegance of exquisite black
on stark white linen cloth.

It couldn't belong to the froth of a laughing girl
for this was black pearl
woman of the world
Chanel
cool witch spell.
It was sex
titillation practised, well-versed
its touch would be midnight enchantment
seductive embrace
Chantilly lace.
It would be ...

I turned to the stair
drawn to her
wanting her, the lady of the glove.

When I reached the floor
nothing was there to be seen
nothing had been.
Yet a fragrance sighed light on the air, a delicate zephyr
a touch
soft as a finger brush
over bare skin
evaporating that stir in me
the her in me
to the ache within.

Daur

It's an "afore it's ower late" raucheness
frae the brave new hip
a loupin intil ilka day
thankrife
a waukenin frae the deid.

It's the clim
doon that crag face
aside a linn o watter
reamy as the veil o a bride
win'-skiffed,
soople rodden brainches for the rope
tae dreep ye -
a hingin swingin spider on its threid -
intil a warld o emerald moss
an stern-white dots o sourock
ablow trees
whaur e'en the air ye breathe is faerie green
an the river narrows run
as rich an broon
as yer life-bluid, through Earth's vein ...

The cove is in there
secretfu' as yer ain soul
gey near beyont the reach
whaur a smeddum unbekennt tae ye
is bidin, deep.

Angels of the North

Like silken Chinese kites
all white luminosity
against summer blue
the gulls are carried forward on a stir of air
inside the still, taut framework
of their bones.
No flapping wings
for high mandarins,
they glide with languid grace
careless lords
of the vast element of space
that is the domain of powerful ones
under the sky's dome.

And men, too, reach for the sky
as mighty ones
and build out on their arms to make them wings
and fly ,
silver angels of the north
launched forth
towards infinity
to roam among planets
and aim in incandescent flame
towards stars.

Guilt

A black Scots Presbyterian bile
that swills aboot yer gut;
the speerit o John Knox
that pints a fingur at yer neb
efter ye've laughed ower much;
the voice o admonition in yer lug
the echo in yer heid
that says "Repent ye o yer sins
or else ye'll pay
for yer misdeeds."

But maist o us
are no juist black eneuch
for sic redress.
Oor sins are mair the grey o thochtlessness
guilt glossed ower.
frae us tae the folk we hurt
a ruefu' smile
a haun's touch

Circles

The earth child gathered stones from clear rock pools
on the island shore
stones
that had been storm-bruised to smoothness
large enough to lie inside her hand
silk-cold
with fingers curled to hold.
She placed them in a widening spiral
on the sand
until there was a circle to dance round
a whorl of stones
like a sculpture from the ancient days
in colour blends of all the earthen tones
creams and gold and pinks and browns and greys.

And as the earth child danced
the circle of the earth whirled round her eyes
and she was housed within the circle dome of skies
and seagulls circled on a current of the air
above her head
and on the sea the circle of the sun was resting
like a ball of red.
And so the child had knowledge of the circles of the earth
as she danced round her timeless Druid ring
and time itself danced round the child
in circles
birth to death
summer, autumn, winter,
and then spring,
summer, autumn, winter,
and the spring.

Journeys

It pleased me
that my foot slipped in to the ancient carved-out shape
as though the shape was moulded
just for me
and fitted
perfectly.

Now I was a lady of the tribe
a chosen one
given grace
to be an elder.

I'd climbed Dunadd alone.
It was the test.
Today, no dripped blood in the votive cup
just up the steep cliff path
past fear
of vertigo and cracked bone
and now my foot was in the mark
and I'd come home
from some sore, driven journey of the soul
whole.

Below
the swallows darted.
The inner dictates of their bodies
have charted airways for them.
All the worlds of sea and moor and marsh
stretch wide
and on the far outside,
Mountains.

After Dunadd
Where to go?

Snowdrops

A glacier of flowers is drifting
Down the drive
At the Conveth.
I collaborated with the earth
To get it going.
Knowing that it might become a whiteness
A delicate stream of lightness
Among the bare trees
of March.

From a paltry planting at the hill's crown
The springlet of snow spilled over,
Feeling its way down,
Imperceptibly moving,
Frothing and creaming and creeping,
Reaching out pale-petalled fingers
Over the brown-ness of the ground
Sliding around the wine-satined bark
Of the wild cherry-gean,
Slipping its tendrils between the beech and the rowan
And the larch.

Twenty years
Since I knelt and felt warmness inside the earth
And listened to the pulsing of the heart of it,
Touched the blooming on the skin of it
Injected life-seed into the core of it
Set in motion my river of flower-snow.

It's growing
And growing,
Flowing past my time.

John Elford

The Third Estate

Part One: Without memories you are nothing

Chapter 1: Great Western Road, Glasgow, Scotland

<u>January 2004</u>

It was dark and it was raining, and Frank Burns knew he was going to die in the next few minutes. He had been sitting on the plastic bench in the bus shelter half way along Great Western Road hoping to catch the last bus home to his dingy ground floor flat.

Although it was dark and deserted, the odd car flashed by and caught him just for a moment in the headlights. He wondered if anyone would stop to help him. As soon as that thought had entered his head he knew he was kidding himself. Help him! Slumped down on his plastic seat, his dirty wet coat hiding his thin undernourished puny body and the long filthy sodden scarf wrapped around him turning him into an unwanted package rather than a person. Thin spindly legs covered by some very distressed old blue jeans and his feet wrapped within trainers that had turned yellow-grey with age. He thought he looked like a senile Doctor Who. He smiled, wishing he could step into a police box with a nubile teenage girl and zoom off into the future or the past, anywhere away from Glasgow.

His throat was on fire, and the Jack Daniels he drank from his flask was not helping. His right hand trembled with emotion. Tears stung his eyes as the images of dead and injured sailors came back to haunt him. All of that had happened such a long time ago down in Bluff Cove. He would always remember the thick black smoke. It hung like a vortex of evil over his ship.

He had been a young man in his early thirties then, and handsome too, at least that was what Kirsty had told him all those years ago.

How old was he now, he wondered. Fifty five, fifty six? He didn't know. He didn't care. He had loved Glasgow once, he had loved Kirsty once. Kirsty was gone and his Glasgow had vanished. This clean Glasgow, this city of culture with its shopping malls, internet cafes and call centres was alien to him.

114

He was sure it used to be a dirty but friendly city. He remembered this bus stop. This is where he would board the green and orange double-decker and clutching Kirsty by the hand they would climb the stairs to the top deck and cuddled up together, sharing greasy chips wrapped up in yesterday's Scotsman or Herald. That was when people liked him, and bus conductors would give him a friendly wink.

No bus conductors now, just sullen pay as you enter drivers, who drove very clean Swedish-engineered ivory coloured buses, striped candyfloss pink and blue. First Bus, what the hell name was that? Then there were the shops - Tesco, Boots, Starbucks all the same, everywhere the same on the shop-lined roads of Glasgow, Manchester or Leeds.

All the same, he still loved the city. He loved the University Buildings, the Museums, the Art Gallery, the Kings Theatre, Lauder's Bar and of course the mighty River Clyde. Some things were still in place, some things you still couldn't fuck with.

Yes the bus drivers hated him, they glared at him, and they didn't want him on their nice tidy buses. He could not remember the last time anyone smiled at him, not that he fucking cared. The young woman in WH Smith who viewed him with contempt, as he fumbled in the pockets of his long coat to find enough loose change to buy the Mirror. The minor panic he invoked when by mistake and in a drunken daze he had tried to buy a bottle of cheap gin from Blockbusters Videos, instead of the Off Licence next door.

Suddenly he remembered, someone *had* smiled at him. When was it now, back in August? Yes, she was about forty and very elegant. He had been resting on a park bench. Just resting, not begging. He would rather starve than beg. He resided in a small flat and had a small pension to live on. After paying the rent, gas and electric there wasn't much left for clothes and food, but he got by somehow. The woman had leaned over him and pushed something into his hand. It was then he caught the whiff of her perfume. *L'air du Temps*. Kirsty had worn *L'air du Temps*. He sighed, remembering her lacy white lingerie that she would wear on those special nights. He sighed again, thinking back to the seventies and eighties. They had been his golden years, when he was married and living with Kirsty.

"Go buy yourself a huge meal," the woman had whispered to him in a rich Texan accent, as she pushed four crisp twenty pound notes into his hand. He had not replied but just stared back at her in amazement. Eighty pounds, had she any idea what she had just given him? Part of him wanted to hand it back, after all he had not asked for anything. He must have looked a sight though, for her to be so generous.

While he debated what to do, she had gone, swept up by other American and Japanese tourists. So that night he had brought a Chinese takeaway and a bottle of claret back to his flat. Pouring out his wine, he had smiled, and holding up his glass he had said aloud, "God bless America."

Now though, he was in deep shit. It was late and he was alone apart from a group of youths in hoodies that were heading towards him. They were laughing and shouting obscenities at passing cars. They had their mobile phones, the newer versions that could double up as cameras. Frank was aware of and impressed by modern technology. It was wasted on these morons, he thought. What he could have done with a decent camera when he was nineteen. Nice soft focus shots of Kirsty. Nude shots; artistic shots, nothing pornographic. Nature shots, like Kirsty by the sea at Largs playing with their collie. What was that dog called? Benn, that was it, after Tony Benn of course. What did these kids do now, oh yes texting each other. He would have text'd Kirsty love poems. He used to write poems to her in a red notebook. He kept it hidden from her, until one day she had found it in his pocket and had read it. He still blushed now at the thought of it. She had gone very quiet and given him a funny look.

That night they had stayed at her Aunt's house in Largs, and she had taken him to her bed, held him and stroked his naked body. It was there with her that he had lost his virginity. He was twenty, she was twenty three. After two serious relationships Kirsty was experienced in the art of love. What Frank lacked in experience he had soon made up for in wild passion. Kirsty had been his only love. His mistress was the Royal Navy and the sea. Until of course the Sky Hawks had attacked. Then for Frank everything had changed.

"Watch where yer walking, you fucking drunk."

The first youth slapped him around the head and he spun and crashed to the ground in a heap. He heard the others jeering, "Kick his head in Andy", someone said.

He knew this would happen, he had known five minutes ago when he had first seen them. He also knew they would kill him. He could have hidden from them. He could have run away when he first saw them. As a fist smashed at his kidneys, he wondered why he had stayed rooted to this spot. He had plenty of time, he could have got away.

Ten years ago, even five, he could have put them all in hospital. Not now though, he was weak and he knew it must be more than just the drink which drained him.

Gasping for air, laying on the ground in the wet, he remembered their parting at Central Station back in 82. She had held his head between her hands while they waited for the train that would take him to Portsmouth, and war.

"You come back to me Frank, do you hear?" she had said, "and be careful, watch that pride of yours, it will be the death of you."

She knew of course. Nothing escaped those eyes of hers. They were fierce eyes, but eyes that could melt your heart in a moment. Green eyes that held you, that hugged you, like a candle hugs a flame. Her eyes could dance and light up the world, children loved her, dogs trusted her, and cats sought out her lap and purred out their affection for the girl with the emerald eyes. Yes, pride had made him stay. He would not run, no matter what the price.

The second kick was to the head, and he felt the warm blood on his neck, he knew they were filming this on their mobiles. Soon his death would be shown in full colour on the net. It was of course extremely unlikely that these young people would ever be caught or convicted, but if they were, the lawyers would have hundreds of excuses for them. Frank knew this as he lay still, losing blood and dying slowly. But he didn't care, he welcomed death. As he heard them swearing, he wondered where all that hate came from. Inwardly he smiled, they will be old one day, sooner than they think, how will they die he wondered. Four more kicks crashed into his limp body and he groaned feebly, wrapping his hands around his head.

The moron called Andy pulled back the sleeve of his left hand to remove the blade from his pocket, revealing the ample supply of coarse black hair which almost hid the strap of his Rolex watch. Just above the watch in vivid green was the tattoo of an Eagle about to drop from the skies to kill its prey. His short fat fingers found the blade and flicked it open. Andy was excited now and felt an uncomfortable stiffness in the crutch of his tight jeans.

Frank had been one of the lucky ones, he had come back. Come back to Glasgow, back to his Kirsty. He was wounded but his wounds were invisible and his body was unmarked. Sometimes he wanted to talk about his ship, but never could. Instead he hugged her tightly. They had picnics on the banks of Loch Lomond, He bought a second hand Cortina and they drove out to Largs and paddled in the sea. Once they had driven to Skye with Benn and spent the nights under canvas to the sound of waterfalls, and he had tried to paint her.

Looking at his masterpiece she had screamed with laughter, "don't give up your day job just yet," she had said and ruffled his mop of blonde hair.

They had been together over twenty happy years and married for most of that time. Frank could not believe his good fortune, while other people he knew suffered the trauma of divorce, his marriage seemed to grow stronger with each passing day. Then, and it was so quick, was the cancer, her emerald eyes dulled and she was gone in months. He stumbled on somehow. Dead end job followed dead end job, bus driver, barman, waiter, even a bouncer when he was still fit, before the drink took hold. Now there was only the Jack Daniels and the telly to dull the senses. The nightmare of Bluff Cove followed him into sleep and he woke in a cold sweat hugging the pillow praying that when he opened his eyes Kirsty would be there. But of course she never was.

Frank was tired now, he wanted the pain to end, and he wanted to die. 'God, if you exist make it stop and give me peace,' he thought. Then as if his prayer had been answered, the pain went and he was floating above the bus shelter looking down on his body, watching as the hoodies continued to film and kick him. Andy cursed and the kicking ceased as the yobs stood aside while Andy delivered the coup de gras and the blade was pushed in deep and then twisted into Frank's guts. Frank was beyond pain now and his spirit was drawing away from his tired crumpled bleeding body.

Above him was a bright light and he felt himself drawn to it. He was moving faster and faster through a dark spiral spinning tube and at the end was the clear white light.

He rushed towards that light it held something for him akin to love. He wanted to embrace the light and feel its intensity. It seemed to swallow him whole and then it left him feeling refreshed and pain free, better than he had ever felt before.

This was incredible, all his life he had been an atheist. If he was honest that was not the whole truth. Because the weak side of him as Frank saw it, still yearned and hoped for more after death.

His mind had convinced him from boyhood that life or the conscience state was a temporary thing before the great nothingness that consumed all human and animal life at the point of death. Science seemed to support this view. Life appeared to Frank as short, brutal, fearful and pointless.

Yet his heart and his emotions longed for something, he did not know what, but something, surely there was something. Something akin to love or beauty, these were the only two things he wanted to cling to.

The wonder and fragrance of a red rose, the inevitability of a rainbow after both sun and rain had teased a bright blue sky. He remembered a holiday he had taken with Kirsty in Yugoslavia before that beautiful country was ripped apart by civil war. They had parked their hired Fiat next to a lush green meadow and watched in wonder as four grey Lipizzaner horses galloped past their white manes and tails like trails of smoke against a background of green leaves and blue sky. The power and spirit of these majestic beasts mocked any notion that they were just a product of evolution and natural selection. No they were made to transport the gods.

Then there was love. First his mother, a busy fussy woman but a good person who had given him values to live by. On reflection she had been undemonstrative and sometimes cold, but he had loved her all the same. It was only when he met Kirsty he realized just how much he needed physical affection and how much he had missed it in his boyhood life. He had lost his mum just after his thirteenth birthday. It was then he stopped talking to his maker. He had loved his father very much, especially so after his mother's death, but in a strange remote kind of way. Ian was a generous man yet emotionally even colder than his mother and Frank was unable to bond with him in the way he had wished.

Next there had been Kirsty, the great love of his life. She was the jewel in his crown, both love and beauty together - his twin reasons for living. When she too had been taken from him, he had become bitter and in many a drunken rage cursed God, other times he had felt an ice cold calm rage and he cursed life itself.

Had he loved others? He had to think hard now rejecting those he had a liking or affection for, that was not love. Others he had loved, his young niece, Jane who he had bounced on his knee. He smiled as he thought of her, yes she had been special. He had loved her. There had been his English Aunt Katie and her daughter Amanda when he was a much younger, but then they had lost touch. While in the navy there had been his best mate Richard but after events down in the South Atlantic, even that close friendship had suffered.

Who else was there? No one he realized. He felt ashamed, so few people in a lifetime. Was he cold like his father? He wondered. There was of course, Benn, Kirsty's collie. Could you love a dog? He could, he did. Remembering Benn's cold wet nose, his innocent but trusting brown eyes. The loyal devotion he showed to Kirsty. Yes he had loved, Benn dog or not.

So that was it, the sum total of meaningful relationships. He felt pain, just when he thought all pain was over forever. A sharp head pain and a vision of a lovely young girl with long dark almost black hair, "Isabelle" he groaned, his older sister. This was mad he had no siblings! Yet the vision was strong and feelings of great love pulled at his heartstrings, then it left him as quickly as it had come.

He felt elated his logical mind had cheated him. He was dead, but this was not the end. A new worry swept over him, if there was a God after all how would he be judged, would he go to hell. Did hell exist after all?

The brilliant white light was a comfort and seemed to indicate he was going to a better place than he had left. It was then his peaceful contentment ended. He was pushed or guided into another tube, this pathway was cold and grey and he was hurling into it at great speed.

He felt sick and frightened was this hell he thought, was this the endless suffering where non believers would have to spend the rest of eternity. Would the fire and brimstone and the angels of Satan be waiting to meet him.

Inwardly he screamed out in terror, "God, please forgive me," and somewhere in his mind a voice answered him.

"Sorry Frank, god has left the building."

Lies, Lust and Loneliness

Why did I lie to my mistress so fair?
To tell her, that I really did care.

Why am I so very alone?
Hoping and praying my wife will phone.

Why did I betray my wife's trust?
For the fruit of forbidden lust.

Why did my daughter slap my face?
When I left home in utter disgrace.

Why did my mistress, so dare?
To find a young man, and complete my nightmare.

Why did my boss decide I must go?
I really, really would like to know.

Mum, Me and the Monster

From the age of two, my boyhood years were spent in the market town of Guildford in Surrey, just thirty miles south west of London.

I am sure I don't remember much before the age of four, but it was about that time the hideous monsters came into my life and I remember every detail about them. These early memories were before I started school, so I must have been four at the most. The monsters were cunning and cruel and lived somewhere in my bedroom.

At night after mum and dad had gone to bed and the house was dark and quiet, I lay in my small bed frozen in fear, knowing they would come for me. It was no good calling out for dad, he would either laugh or tell me in his gruff voice to go to sleep. Mum was more understanding. If I called her she would sigh, but would always give me a cuddle before returning to her room. The monsters of course knew this. They would just wait for mum to calm me down, fetch me a drink and place a small night light in my room. Once she had gone, they would begin their campaign of terror.

If there was a night light in my room, it would cast shadows which were comforting to begin with because I was petrified of the dark, but that comfort would not last for long. Soon the shadows would take on terrible shapes which would acquire scary faces with glowing eyes and they would stare back at me. Then I would shut my eyes trying so hard to blot out the demons which filled my room.

Once asleep, they would follow me into my dreams. I once felt a tap on my shoulder and thinking it must be mum, I opened my eyes to meet a most hideous sight that I still recall to this very day. The thing stood next to my bed. It had scales like a fish and stood upright like a person on two legs.

In this nightmare, this ghoul stank. The smell was gut retching, a sickly sweet odour mixed with a cocktail of burnt rubber and bad eggs. It had three eyes. Two were on insect like stems and the third eye was in the centre of a face full of ugly warts, rotten skin and scales. Red, swollen and diseased, it stared down at me. Then I was sick, all over the sheets and blankets and I screamed for mum yet again.

Mum I remember was especially nice to me despite the mess I had made on the bedding. I was sure she just thought it was a stomach upset. I was far too young and inarticulate to describe the fear that the vision had given me.

My god those monsters were clever though, as soon as my bedroom light flashed on and mum entered the room, they vanished. If only mum could catch one red-handed, then she would know I was telling the truth. One day she would see them I was sure and she would know what to do, because my mum knew everything.

Sometimes mum would even crawl under my bed to convince me they were not hiding there. I realised that, as horrible as these monsters were, they must be scared of mum because they always hid from her.

Little did I know it would not be long before mum did catch one of them and then my life would change forever and I would be free of them at last.

This all happened in Woking station in broad daylight, which was strange as monsters had never bothered me in the daytime before and I suppose this is where they made their big mistake.

Back in those days, only rich people had cars and our family went everywhere on buses or trains. We had relatives in Woking, which is about ten miles away from Guildford. One day Mum. Dad and I boarded the Southern Region green Electric Train, which trundled its way at a sedate speed to Woking. I was used to this form of transport, but I do remember how boring and slow these Electric Trains were. There was some small excitement for a small boy like me when a Goods Train passed us. The Goods Trains were pulled by small Steam Engines, much more interesting than those dull Electric Trains.

I remember on that day a Goods Train passed us pulling, it seemed to me, an endless number of trunks filled to the brim with coal. Right at the back was the guard's van, which was so much like a giant version of my clockwork train set.

When we reached Woking and stepped out on to the platform, some people dad knew saw us and had a long talk to my parents. I was bored with all this adult conversation and wandered down the platform. Woking station was bigger than the station at Guildford with many more platforms and trains.

I remember too there were a fair number of pigeons at the end of platform 2 and I walked down to investigate them. By now, I was a fair distance from my parents and they had not noticed how far I had wandered.

As I looked along the railway track, I saw a dark shape away in the distance. As I stared, the dark shape got larger and then I could see a plume of white steam above it and I smiled. Another Goods Train I thought and moved nearer to the edge of the platform for a better view.

The railway track was making a strange noise. It was like a hollow rumbling and it was getting louder. At that moment, the Goods Train let out a strange hooting noise together with large amounts of white steam. 'Goodness,' I thought, 'this seems to be a rather large Goods Train and it's moving so very fast.'

Now I could see it clearly even though there was so much steam. It was huge, awesome. The Engine looked so very different to the small steam Engines I was used to, it was smooth and streamlined and it was coming straight at me at a terrible speed.

I heard a longer and shriller hoot, hoot, as it flew into Woking Station.

All the little waiting rooms and small shops on Platform 2, shook as if an earthquake was about to hit. I screamed in terror expecting at any moment to feel the impact of this steam driven monster. But it did not hit me, it missed me by inches. Next came a blur of brown and cream streaks of colour, which I discovered much later on were just the Pullman Carriages of the non-stop Express from London to Bournemouth, better known as the "Bournemouth-Belle".

Those brown and cream streaks were as frightening as the crazed Engine and they tried to suck me into their metallic embrace, and so I screamed again and as quickly as the monster had appeared it had gone and my mother's arms were around me, as I sobbed into the shoulder of her coat.

"Did you see it mum?" I cried.

"Yes", she said, "you were standing too close to the edge of the platform John. I've told you so many times about that".

She had seen the monster and it had not dared to harm me. I suddenly felt so much better, the monsters are scared of my mum I thought and although they might scare me sometimes, nothing really bad would happen to me.

From that day on, the monsters left me alone and I slept soundly night after night, knowing that my mum was the monster's monster.

Bobby Lauder

Dinnertime

The dinner it was ready
the wife she put it out
then she went to the door
to give her man a shout

She saw him in the garden
standing staring into space
His mucky pipe was in his mouth
and a smile was on his face

Five times she shouted to him
and five times she was ignored
She thought she'd try it one more time
 this time she really roared

Then this short-sighted woman
 went out to bring him home
'twas only then she realised
'twas her new gigantic gnome

Coro-neigh-tion Street

Our pony Major, small and sweet
he dotes on Coronation Street
and when he hears the music play
from his warm stable he will stray

He often kicks upon our door
he'll kick until his hooves are sore
and when the door is opened wide
our proud pony steps inside

Carrots are lying in the room
they're there for Major to consume
he's so bossy as we all know
and sulks if he should miss a show

On the couch he'll watch the telly
while he's filling up his belly
he knows he is amongst his friends
and waits until the programme ends

And our poor Major couldn't cope
if we should ban him from the soap
our cuddly pony small and sweet
is hooked on Coronation Street

Doo Widow

Whaur's ma hubby? Oh, can't ye tell?
In his doo hut aw by himsel
'Tween brekfast time an time fur tea
that man o mine ah hardly see

He said he luv'd me tae he could burst
But noo he says his doos come first
Maist folk hae weans wi airms an legs
Bit aw his sprogs come oot o eggs

The bugger never thinks o me
when he's in his 'maternity'
He oaftin nurses the scraggy things
an tries tae mend their broken wings

He gave his weddin band tae me
when ah wis only twinty three
An noo amangst the muck an eggs
the rings go oan his pigeons' legs

Ah'm lonely when we're no the gither
Ah wisny boarn wi wings an feathers
Oaften he his tae hide his face
as his birds hae never won a race

Nae wunner he is getting thinner
As he is seldom doon fur dinner
Oh, whaur's ma hubby? Can't ye tell?
Up in his doo hut aw by himsel

Heart of a Child

As she was sitting on a swing, the girl, she sucked an ice,
The park was very busy and the flowers they looked so nice
The wind was blowing on her back, the sun was on her face,
But this girl of forty years, she looked so out of place.

She had an operation and received a young girl's heart
it seems as if her tedious life has had a brand new start
she's often playing marbles along with all the boys
and this girl is often seen with little girlie toys

She's often playing at peevers, she's a conker queen as well
And in her brand new outfit, that girl, she feels just swell.
She's often chasing all the birds, by climbing up the trees
And ripping all her dresses, or skinning both her knees.

This girl, she likes hamburgers, she likes ice lollies too,
And whenever this girl swears, the air is always blue,
She's always full of mischief, and she feels young and wild,
But this lass of forty years owns the warm heart of a child.

Jenny's Babe

When Jenny's babe refused to come
the doc knew what to do
He thought he would entice it out
with a can of Barr's Irn Bru
When he showed the babe the can
it stretched out a tiny hand
the wee mite was so thirsty
that it didn't understand

As the babe it grabbed the can
doc was concerned for Mum
as he leant across her bed
and listened to her tum
Soon he heard a gurgling
as the drink the babe did shift
and as the can flew in the bin
he could hear a mighty rift.

Oops! Sorry Miss!

As Debbie she sat in the class
the girl she felt a fool
as she'd just wet her knickers
in her first week at school

The teacher said, 'Don't worry, dear'
stroking her golden hair
'Just you go into the toilets and
put on this other pair.'

The little girl she left the class
and did as she was told
and when she went to change herself
the toilets felt so cold.

When she gave hers to the teacher
she tried to hide her sin
As the teacher took them from her
she tossed them in the bin.

'You can bring them back tomorrow,'
the teacher she did say
then once she tidied up her books
the girl went out to play.

When she came back in the morning
the sun was shining bright
As she met all her little friends
she was filled with delight.

As her dad he stopped the car
he opened up the door
and Debbie joined the boys and girls
as she had done before.

And when she saw her teacher there
her friends stood round about
'Miss, your knickers are in Dad's pocket,'
that little girl did shout.

Wrong Feet

When Harry put his slippers on
and came walking in the door
his mum was disappointed
as she looked down at the floor

'They are on the wrong feet,' she said
when the error she did spot,
her lad, he said, 'How can they be?
They're the only feet I've got.'

Lilias Michael

The Princess of Eternal Peace

Ch. 1: Beware a dagger hidden in a smile. (Shi Nai-an, Ming)

Yung-T'ai sighed and rising from the small backless chair, walked over to the window, and looked down on the courtyard below. Occasionally she was allowed to walk around in the fresh air, accompanied by her aunt or Su Lin, her personal maidservant, but never in all her sixteen years had she been outside the palace. Many times she had wondered what lay beyond the high walls and towers. She knew there was another world, having heard stories from the older ladies in the women's quarters, those who, in their youth had been escorted by husbands, now departed to the gods, to functions given by high-ranking officials having their own houses in the city besides grace-and-favour apartments in the Imperial Palace. Confined to their own apartments, the other female members of the T'ang royal family and the concubines were only brought into contact with the men at their bidding, so the world for them was restricted. Topics of conversation scarcely rose above the gossip and intrigues of the close society in which they lived, but at times memories would surface and tales of mad carriage rides through the streets of the city at dead of night, when high spirits of youth were only curtailed as the horses approached the Palace gates, had Yung-T'ai breathless with excitement.

'Oh, if only I could ride in a carriage throughout the city streets!'

Being a princess was no escape. But she had been born with an inquisitive nature, a sense of the ridiculous in the pomp of the female hierarchy around her and an ability to instil loyalty amongst the servants who attended her. Sometimes when she hinted that she wished to wander around the palace, doors would be opened by shadowy figures in long black flowing robes, then quickly disappear as silently as they had come. Not that they went far. She knew their eyes were upon her, following her every movement and when danger loomed, the click-clicking of their tongues would signal them to gather around, hiding her, and slowly, as if going about their normal business, escort her back to the women's quarters. These escapades had not been without some excitement as she crept through the long passages, and her inquisitive ear had gathered gossip she knew she ought not to have heard. Her heart would beat wildly at the thought of being discovered, but it became a game she and the servants played. A game that could result in tragedy, but the sheer adrenalin rush affected them too, and once they were all back they would laugh and giggle in sheer relief that once again they had come out unscathed.

Now she was waiting in this ante-room, feeling alone and uncertain. She had never been here before and looking round the walls was aware of the exotic paintings of flowers and birds. With the lattice shutters open the afternoon sun bathed each one in a warm glow, enhancing the artist's colours of vermilion, jade green, sapphire blue and yellow. At any other time she would have been happy to look carefully at each one, admiring or criticising form and brush stroke for she knew there was a new artist appointed to the court who had been doing work in the royal apartments. Her education had been scanty but it had not neglected the finer subjects which all ladies of the Royal family were expected to learn. But today was different. She was waiting to be called into the large throne room where her fate would be determined. Art was far from her mind.

The message had been brought to her while she was eating with the other women and girls in the dining room that morning. One of the senior servants spoke to her through an oval hole in the door.

'Princess Yung-T'ai, His Highness, your uncle requests that you make yourself ready to be presented to Her Royal Highness, Empress Wu, this afternoon to make arrangements for your marriage. He tells you to dress appropriately as befits a princess. And not to speak unless spoken to.' These last words had been said louder than the rest, and Yung-T'ai knew this was for the benefit of the other women who were listening intently. She knew also that for this brief moment he felt superior. They were only women, of no great importance, whereas he was a man and had a most important job to do. Anger rose within her at his presumption but curbing it, she had answered sweetly and politely.

'Thank you, Tsui- san. Please tell my uncle I shall be there.'

'I shall come to escort you, so be ready,' he said authoritatively and turned away.

Yung-T'ai had made a face at his back and returning to the table, was confronted by the twittering ladies of the house of women, eyes agog. Amongst them was her aunt, sister of her father. She had been mainly responsible for nurturing the Princess during the past few years since her mother died. The father, Chung-tsung, elder son of the Empress and legitimate heir to the Chinese throne, had been deposed within months of his succession by his mother, and later sent to a remote part of the city where her spies made sure he had no access to government affairs. Yung-T'ai had been too young to know or understand what happened, but she felt the absence of both parents deeply, and without brothers or sisters, life could be lonely at times.

'My dear, this is a great moment,' the aunt said. 'You have the chance to become a very important married lady, with a luxurious home of your own, many servants and rich gowns and jewels. And if you produce a son, your future will be even more brilliant. Oh, if only I were younger!' Her plump homely face had crumpled and tears came into her eyes. Yung-T'ai knew some of her aunt's history. It was said that once she had had a suitor, but he disappeared mysteriously, giving rise to the rumour that he had been executed for daring to make rude comments upon the features of the Empress, whose beauty had vanished with the years. Whether this was true or not, Tai-ping had never married. Now it was the Princess's turn to be wooed, but was she ready? It seemed only yesterday she had been playing with the other children in the harem and now the Empress was to decide her fate and future. Suddenly she had felt cold.

'Yes, Aunt, I know it is my duty to marry well, and I am excited to meet the man who is to be my husband.' Yung-T'ai had said these words in as cheerful a voice as she could manage, but deep inside her heart was heavy. She was about to make a marriage arrangement with a stranger, an arrangement concocted between her grandmother and her uncle, Jui-tsung. He was a weak and ineffectual Crown Prince, no match against his mother. She dominated China, ruling with a tyrannical fervour that terrorised the population, and made no differences as far as family was concerned. The merits of several would-be suitors had been discussed, some of whom looked upon marrying Yung-T'ai as a means of furthering their advance into the royal household, but it was Wu's decision that mattered and she had selected a commander of the second rank of Imperial Carriages. He was a high born member of the Tang court, eminently suitable to be the husband of a princess, *and surely there's no chance of Yung-T'ai ever becoming empress,* as that formidable female kept assuring herself. The fact that he was somewhat older than the Princess, a widower with sons, scarcely mattered.

'He'll be a steady influence. Curb that flightiness in her!' she'd said to Jung-tsung, who had nodded his agreement, as he did to most of her suggestions.

The Princess had taken great care over her appearance, with the help of Su Lin, and by mid-afternoon was waiting to be summoned to the throne room. Her best dress was of rich green silk, the skirt long and narrow. The bodice and sleeves were full, to conceal her womanliness, and her jet-black hair piled high above her forehead, secured by a jade comb. As a young unmarried girl, her jewellery was scant. Only a long gold chain round her neck, holding the figure of a jade Buddha. She was young, beautiful, on the threshold of life, and in the next few hours that life would be put into the hands of a stranger.

The large doors opened and Tsui-san, accompanied by another servant, approached. They bowed and Tsui-san said,

'Princess, Her Royal Highness the Empress is ready to see you now. Please come with us.'

One on either side, they escorted her into the long throne room, their feet in soft flat shoes making a gentle swish as they half-ran, half-slid along the floor, propelling Yung-T'ai towards her destiny. With heart fluttering, she looked at the door and slowly it opened.

****

She sat in the high-backed royal throne, a slight wizened figure, dressed in robes befitting an Empress. A gown made from the best silk worms that China produced and of a golden hue that would outshine the sun if it were ever allowed to penetrate these walls, devoid of windows. A few stray grey hairs escaped from the edges of an incongruous black wig rising above her head like an enormous thumb mark, as if to say, 'This is my stamp of authority. Ignore it at your peril!' Atop this her dressers had placed a gold circlet encrusted with rubies, diamonds and semi-precious stones, the whole effect being spoiled by it slipping drunkenly to one side. But then she was the Empress and no one had the temerity or courage to bring this fact to her notice.

Apart from her lined painted face, the only other parts of her skin to be seen were her gnarled hands with their long nails grasped round the carved dragon heads at the ends of the chair arms. Her eyes were closed and to an observer it might appear that she was asleep. Certainly for the court officials and visitors surrounding her it was so, for not a word or whisper passed their lips. To do so would have amounted to treason, and they all knew the penalty for upsetting Empress Wu. Banishment from Court, life exile, and even the ultimate "chop" or convenient hushed-up murder had been fairly common events since this crone had usurped the throne and ruled with tyranny and fear. So the men around her, and they were all men, kept their feelings hidden. Not even amongst themselves could they express anger or hatred towards this female despot for fear of being overheard by one of her many spies. And there was one figure seated alongside the Empress, as one of equality, who would not hesitate to betray any of them, family or not. This was Shangguan Wa'ner, the only other female in the assembly. As a young concubine she had found favour with the monarchy when she had shown her intelligence and educational skills and was soon writing imperial edicts for Wu. She became head of the Palace harem and, most importantly, Wu's eyes and ears to the gossip and intrigues that circled around the court.

Seated on a low chair, slightly behind her, in deference to his mother's august position, was Jui-tsung, Crown Prince. He was no match for his older brother now languishing in exile, but had no desire for their fortunes to be reversed. Hence his willingness to acquiesce in all her commands and decisions.

But the Empress was not asleep. Opening her eyes, she stretched out the long fingers, made longer by nails which had been sharpened into dagger-like points, then relaxed them and drew her hands into her lap.

'Gentlemen, I think my granddaughter is arriving. Let us greet her with the respect she is due.'

They all looked towards the door at the far end of the throne room, which was slowly opening. Then three figures appeared; a servant on either side of the Princess. Wu's eyes narrowed as she watched every movement of Yung-T'ai's progress. It had been some time since she last saw her granddaughter and the girl's emergence into womanhood took the aged Empress by surprise. For one split second she felt fear, but that turned to hatred and envy as she acknowledged Yung-

T'ai's youth and beauty. Her mouth tasted the bile which rose up from within and it took a great effort to keep from shouting, 'No, no, take her away! Back to the other women.'

Inside the words were different.

Oh, I hate her youth. I hate her lineage. She'll have everything on a golden plate, not have to fight for favours, fight to survive as I've had to do. And once she's a married woman will she try to take over? I don't trust her. I don't trust anyone, least of all a beautiful girl like her.

The small black eyes seemed to reflect her thoughts for the Princess faltered as she neared the throne. They showed no warmth and she shivered, trying hard not to look into those dark forbidding pools which appeared to bore into her very soul. Not a word was said for several heart-stopping seconds. The men around held their breath as if in a spell, but their eyes grew large in anticipation of what was to come. Then the deep red lips parted: a mere slit in a whit painted face. Wu, in a voice barely above a whisper, croaked,

'Well, Yung-T'ai, I see you have grown up since I saw you last. Your Aunt has done well by you and you seem a pretty young lady. Is that not so, Wan'er?'

A thin smile and a slight nod of the head was the only answer. Shangguan was confident in her power.

The words tasted like vinegar in the old woman's mouth but she continued.

'And now it is time for you to marry. Several eligible gentlemen have asked for your hand in marriage, and we have decided that Wang Su, the commander in charge of the Imperial carriages, and of high birth in our court, is to be your husband. You are a very lucky girl, is she not, Jui-tsung?'

This gentleman nodded his head, looking at Yung-T'ai, who stared stonily at him. She had no regard for this interloper as the whole court knew that her father, Chung-tsung, was the rightful Crown Prince, not this weak puppet.

The Empress turned to the group around her and motioned to a tall distinguished man to come forward. Yung-T'ai's first impression was of a fatherly figure, his top-knot showing a preponderance of grey, but there was a certain handsomeness about him that might have appealed to the Princess had she had seen him under other circumstances. This was not one of them. As Wu Yanji approached he looked straight into her eyes, smiling gently, and put forward his hands to take hers. But she, recoiling, put them behind her back. The gentleman stopped in his tracks and looked at the Empress.

'Is she not ready for marriage, your Royal Highness? I was told by your emissaries that she had been prepared to meet me. However, if she is averse to being wed, I am prepared to wait a little longer.'

'Nonsense, of course she's ready,' growled Wu. 'She's just being coy and difficult. She has no father to control her and she needs a steadying hand in a husband of your ability and wisdom.' The Empress's voice became honey-sweet as she added,

'I know you are the man for her. You will be gentle. More like a father than a husband in the beginning, until you have her under your control. She is still a child in many ways, but I see a fire of passion beneath that cold face she is showing us all. Trust me, she will succumb to your will eventually.'

As Yung-T'ai heard these words she cried out,

'No, no, I don't want to marry and certainly not this old man!'

'Old man? What do you mean, you silly child? You want to marry a boy? What could a boy give you except heartache? A boy hasn't finished planting his paddy fields and he looks for new and richer ones besides those at home. I tell you, Yung-T'ai, you WILL take Wu Yanji as your husband, and that is MY final decision!'

'No, never! If my father were here I know he would not push me into a marriage I didn't want. Why can't he be here to help me?'

At these words Wu stood up from the throne, trembling with rage, and pointing one long finger at Yung-T'ai menacingly, shouted,

'Don't ever mention your father to me again! Chung-tsung is a son of mine no longer. He has been disgraced and sent from Our Presence. I could have him killed if I so wished, remember that you stupid little girl. Yanji, pay no attention to her. She will do as I command, so now we shall make all preparations for the nuptials.' Breathing deeply and with great effort to regain her regal stature, she turned to the assembly.

'Gentleman, the meeting is at an end. You,' pointing to the two servants, who had been standing to one side of Yung-T'ai during the procedures, 'escort my granddaughter back to her quarters.' Gathering her robes around her and with as much dignity as her old body would allow, she swept out of the room through the doors behind the throne which had been opened silently as if on wheels, by two large guards. Shangguan and Jui-tsung followed, he almost tripping over his robes in his haste to show his loyalty. The assembly of men, palms of their hands touching, made deep bows towards their retreating figures, and even after the door had closed continued in this manner for a few more seconds. One never knew who was watching after all!

There was a deathly silence. Then gradually murmurs and tutt-tuttings were heard.

'Her Royal Highness is perfectly correct,' piped up a thin reedy voice. 'Young girls must be married off as quickly as possible and they have no say in the matter. She was extremely rude to the Empress. I tell you, you'll have your work cut out to control that termagant. But when you do,' and here he sniggered in thin soprano-like tones, 'I hope the delights will be worth all the trouble!'

Wu Yanji said nothing, only looking at the figure of Yung-T'ai as she was being escorted through the door at the far end of the room. His heart was heavy. Would she ever grow to love him, or even like him? For his part he had felt an attraction the first time he'd glimpsed her through the openings of a secret panel in the wall of the women's sitting room. This was where would-be suitors were allowed to view the young girls before any decisions were made to put forward a proposal of marriage. She had looked so lovely, so young, laughing and playing, that for the first time since his wife had died a few years previously, the thought of being with a woman again excited and thrilled him. He wanted her and knew the Empress's will would prevail, but it saddened him that he would have to fight for Yung-T'ai's respect and eventual acquiescence.

'I think I am perfectly capable of taking on a young girl, even at my age, without reverting to strong man tactics, thank you! Now if you'll excuse me, I have affairs waiting for my attendance, so I bid you farewell, gentlemen,' and with these words he left the room.

'My, he was very high and mighty,' said the reedy-voiced man. 'He'd better marry the girl quickly before she creates trouble. Getting on the wrong side of the Empress can bring dreadful results.' Here he whispered. 'And don't you remember what happened to the late Empress? I heard she'd been killed and then her limbs pickled in wine! But I'm sure that's only a rumour to discredit Her Imperial Majesty.' These words were spoken louder and he looked round fearfully. Spies could be anywhere.

In ones and twos the men left, chattering amongst themselves of all that had taken place. Back in the ante-room Yung-T'ai took one last look from the open window, and then went with the servants to the women's quarters. None of them spoke and she walked as if in a dream, a dream of fear. Her cosy life within these cloistered walls, although restricted, was about to end, and her future seemed dark and indistinct. Who could help her? The other unmarried girls would be envious, she was sure, but she did not wish to be committed to a man old enough to be her father. Opening the door into her apartment, she was confronted by Su Lin who had been waiting anxiously for her return.

'Mistress, has it all been arranged? Are you happy with the choice?'

Yung-T'ai's face crumpled. Tears which had been close to the surface now cascaded down her cheeks, and the servant immediately gave comfort by putting her arms around her and gently drawing her towards the bed.

'Come now, try not to upset yourself. Let me dry your face, then prepare you for this evening's meal.'

'No! I couldn't possibly eat. I just want to put it all behind me and sleep. Maybe when I waken in the morning it will all have been a terrible dream! Please, Su Lin, help me to undress and get into bed, then go down and give my Aunt my apologies for missing the meal, that I am feeling slightly unwell.'

The servant was alarmed at how upset the Princess was, but said nothing more and quietly began preparing her mistress for bed. Once Yung-T'ai was tucked up in the little cot which was all that her grandmother provided for her comfort, she excused herself and left for the dining hall to deliver the message. Yung-T'ai lay under the thin cover, her body trembling as she tried to control her sobbing.

'Oh Pappa, if only you were here with me. To talk to me and give me advice. I need you so, much!'

As a dam bursting, the tears came in deep retching sobs that only ended when, exhausted, she sank into deep sleep.

Maureen Blake

Castle in the Sky

The whistling wind
Awakens me from dreams
laced in rose petals, not of castles in the sky
as many would dream

But of stone and mortar
moat and battlement
with banners flying colourful, against the wild
and warring sky

These gnarled hands
once gathered berries
in the castle grounds, blood red against the golden
glance of autumn

Where once flowers
plucked, not yet dead
adorned a princess' hair, piled high in an auburn crown
and bright with ribbons

Here at Fotheringay
in deep despairing dark
the castle sleeps in shadows cast by wolves, who dream
a Queen will die today

I close my eyes
and flee this place
across the clouded drawbridge, no less than real
To my castle in the sky

Rewind

The Queen's telegram was read
by relatives chatting around my bed
Did I die? Speak up! What?
Oh Eighty now am I, Bah the youth of today
hit them with my stick
At seventy with a body heading south
I'm dancing to heavy metal and, I swear
the younger I get the better I look
Pulled a sixty year old at sixty five
Take me to your jungle baby
Dumped at fifty one, pulled a muscle
yelling "SHE DESERVES HIM".
So this is forty? Well, champagne's fizzing
Cheers then. Do you like jazz?
Thirty five, hello? God no! A broken arm
Shit, and I have to sleep with him again?
Don't answer that for at thirty two
I'm having a good time on the 30th floor
with career on my mind. Lord it's going so fast
So when I ski will I do it backwards?
Thirty and pissed as a fart, that sparkling ring
I'm stuffing down a drainhole with a stick
At twenty seven I'm turning the new key, smiling
As I hold the ring up to catch the moonlight
It's my birthday and I'll cry if I want to
Clinging by painted fingernails at twenty five
from a hot guy's window ledge. Don't ask
Twenty one again, twenty one again
Steamy dancing through a whole LP
Sweet seventeen with hormones jumping
Painted lips mini skirts and heels so high
Help!! Navy knickers and knee-high socks?
The janny's coming *stub it out stub it out*
He pulled my hair he pulled my hair
Ma I wet my pants
Goo goo gah!

A Coup de Grâce

"Is that so?" demanded he,
the steam raising parody of war
and as declarations flash in his eyes
he pauses; loading his attack

She bridges the gap; draws first blood
Savaging his *blah de blah*

His foot beats out a tattoo
A rat-a-tat fuck you; and through teeth
clenched tight, he drops a bomb
blasting at her scorn

Her tongue flicks open the Book of Curses
riddling him chapter and verse

His final foray meets its target; piercing his heart
when from the trenches, her flag emerges
washed emotionally white; as she mourns
his coup de grâce

From the ashes in tattered silence, rises dignity
in sorrowful embrace

One Hot Day

The grass is long and lush and very green. Nine cows graze in this field and one standoffish horse. The horse stands grazing at the furthest corner of the field, offering full view of his rump. He doesn't even turn his head to look at us, although the cows do manage a glimpse apiece, before getting lost once more in their lunch. We straddle the stile facing each other.

"Take the daisies out of your hair Morag."

I love his voice more than his face. It is a strong deep baritone voice. His face on the other hand, is as plain as his name, but God yes, it's his voice that gets me. I smile happily at him, a smile that he does not care to return.

"You look like a fool," he says.

Ah that voice. I do love his voice.

"Lets get butt naked," I say, "and lie down in this very field."

He can hardly contain his rage.

"For God's sake woman," he shouts, "are you wholly mad?"

I swing my other leg over the stile as the laughter burbles up inside me.

"As mad as a hat John Briggs. As mad as a hat."

'Shout again do John,' I silently beseech. He doesn't shout again though. He doesn't say another word as I stand here before him throwing off my clothes. He doesn't even move a muscle. He just sits there on that stile, watching me with an expression that my powers of description cannot do justice to. Shock and horror will just have to do for now.

I lie down in the long cool grass and the sound of busy crickets fill my ears. From the corner of my eye, I see that John stays right where he is. I can just make out his hairy ankle, winking as pale as a winter moon from under his trouser leg. The cows have come over for a good old look though. I knew they would. I lie here staring past their heads and up into the deep blue of the sky. John stays sitting on that stile.

Still, I'm happy. John isn't though. Hell, has he ever smiled or laughed just for the sake of it? Has he ever done anything just for the wild crazy joy of it? Well, not that I know of. Sure, he allows his lips the occasional upward motion, but I can tell by his ankle that he isn't smiling now, oh no.

"That's enough now Morag. You've proved you are shameless. That should be enough for you now."

Hah, that voice. It positively vibrates the earth beneath me and the sky is just a little bit bluer. Here's wishing John would become a little bit bluer too but alas, no. The cows wander off back to their grazing and I hum a little tune, to send them on their way.

Trouble is, you see, John wants to head off and become a man of the cloth. He wants to stand on a pulpit and preach the word of God, using that fine baritone voice of his to fill a church. He longs to prostrate himself before an altar and steep himself in prayers to purge his soul. He wants to do that right now and I know that, even as I lie here, he is calling on all of the saints and God himself to keep his butt on that stile. 'Keep me on this stile oh Lord, even if you have to nail my butt to it.' That's what he's saying, for there sits a man who wants to carry the cross and here lies a girl who is that cross. Why doesn't he know that?

My, the grass is warm on my back. I can hear the swoosh of a car coming along the road on the north side of the field.

"Get up now Morag. Look. Someone's coming."

What a voice. The car passes on and I go back to my meditation and John to his frantic praying.

If John took up the cloth, I wouldn't be part of the picture now, would I? He would be so caught up with his flock that he wouldn't have time to dwell on me and nor would he wish to. I know these things.

A jet streaks across the sky leaving a snow-white trail in its wake. Don't look up at the sky John. I know he is, for his leg moved upwards. Look down at me. Look at me John.

John would like to wear the collar. I saw him through his window practising. He was wearing a black sweater and had a white napkin in his hand. He folded the napkin until it was no more than an inch wide, then he turned to the mirror above the fireplace and clasped the napkin at the back of his neck. As he held it, he moved his head this way and that, critically examining his priestly look.

His mother came into the room at that point and I quickly ducked down beneath the windowsill. I could hear her saying "What are you doing John?" Yes, what are doing John, sitting there on that stile, while I lie here naked in this field?

151

A pretty blue butterfly lands on my nose and then flutters off. I pluck a long blade of grass, stretch it between my two thumbs and blow until the shrill whistle pierces a hole in John's prayer.

"Morag, that is it. I have had enough of your stupidity. I am leaving you here with the cows. No more, do you hear? Enough is enough!"

Ah, the longest outpouring yet, vibrating through the earth and coming right at me.

One day two weeks ago, John almost kissed me. He sat there reading his bible down by the stream and I snuck up behind him and covered his eyes.

He panicked. Shouted, "Who is that?"

I tried not to giggle. "An angel John. That's who I am. Just an angel who jumped right out of the pages of that bible."

Well the very idea of it must have tickled something in him, for he stopped struggling and became quite calm. Then, as fast as a snake, he turned and grabbed me and it was at that moment his lips parted. I guess he must still have been seeing angels, as he leaned towards me. I spoiled everything though, when I reached up and put my arms around his neck. That spooked him and he shook me off and stomped off with his bible under his arm, saying "shame on you Morag."

He moved downstream and sat on another rock and I followed, throwing taunts at him while he pretended to read. But he didn't leave. John wouldn't leave me. I'd bet all the cows in this field and that uncaring horse on that much, for I am his temptation. I am his Eve and as much as he tries not to look at this apple-stealing woman, he will be peeking. I know this.

Reaching out, I pick some more daisies and lace them into my long curly hair. John's liturgy is just about audible now. Frantic whisperings reach me through the long grass and the grass frantically whispers back to him, 'come lie beside Morag oh John."

Two years ago, I spied John in his garden hut reading a magazine. There was a picture of a naked girl on the front of it, that's how dirty it was. Holy John was positively licking his lips then, as I watched him through the grimy window. He sat on a canvas chair facing the window - facing me. Although being glued to the magazine as he was, he didn't notice me watching him. He knew that I had spied him though, when his mother came out of the house yelling,

"You girl. You! Get out of this garden now and don't let me see you here ever again."

She started to run after me then and I banged on the window and snatched another peek at John before scampering off. He was white with fright, what with his mother yelling and me laughing. The fence when I jumped it, caught my dress and ripped it. That old witch!

John has both legs dangling over the stile now. Is he coming to join me? I stand up gently, so as not to shake the daises from my hair. That spooks him. Me standing up like that, and he's off ranting again, telling me to get my clothes back on.

Well now, I love John's voice, but damn it if he hasn't made me angry. I really thought I had him there but alas, no. Mister sanctimonious just can't get off his damn preachy hellfire and damnation arse, to come over here and even meet me halfway.

I turn and put two fingers between my teeth and my piercing whistle finally gets that old horse's attention, for here he comes at a trot. I knew he would. I take hold of his mane and haul myself up and off we canter towards the gap in the hedge.

"For God sake Morag!"

I turn around only to see John running after me and stumbling to pick up my clothes as he goes and he shouts "Give this up Morag. Put your clothes back on."

I kick the horse into a flying gallop.

"Go to hell John Briggs", I yell back, "Go straight to hell."

The Lansdowne Wedding

The bride and groom, for all to see
Burst into blossom
And with voices shedding petals
Vowed their love

Ave Maria echoed high above
In a sky of electric blue
Later, raining showers of laughter
From guests, confetti bright

Buses red and ribbon-decked
Toured the City filled with smiles
From Hampstead to Mayfair
Glowing in wedding light

In the courtyard, voices burbled
In a champagne fountain
Overflowing with speeches
Accolades, giving love its name

And all eternally captive in time's eye
In the sweet smell of petals falling
From a balcony on high
As a bouquet sails the air

To Mike

The years seem to fly by
Faster than six wains on a capoogie
With pram wheels whirring; you
Steering with string

My first memory of you tastes of fruit
Stolen from a snow white cake
Baked for your fifth birthday
Strawberries raided at dawn

I can still taste their sweetness; feel
Our childish glee, at your fiftieth party
The years seem to fly by
Faster than six wains on a capoogie

* Capoogie means go-cart or bogie

Turn Back Time

Most of the tourists had been evacuated from Scotland in their sleep. When they awoke, each and every one had found themselves sitting at a pavement café with a cup of coffee in their respective hands as they watched the sunrise. They could have been in Paris, Barcelona or Amsterdam, but they wouldn't know where until they tasted the coffee.

In the country the tourists had left behind, the thunder of horses' hooves shook the ground as riders in their thousands galloped north, leaving a cloud of dust over the highest of trees and mountains. The smell of horseflesh permeated the very earth and reached the delicate noses of every furry animal in the land, as a warning to run for their lives. Birds rudely awakened, took to the wing screeching out their shock. The country was awake and it was trembling.

Time had not run out in Scotland, it had run in the opposite direction from out. For as Neptune and the descendents held hands and concentrated, in every home as the inhabitants slept, their clocks had run backwards with such speed that they exploded. And as each native awoke before the first crack of dawn, they shuffled sleepily into the past, lighting candles on their way.

Men, some of whom had gone to bed as women or children, now dressed and polished their swords. Then they waited and listened for the sound of bagpipes that would call them to arms.

Outside, their horses were tethered in readiness. Some of those horses turned their eyes to the skies and neighed an entreaty for their former lives. Others snorted in thanks to their maker for the good luck of their new and handsome form. By the time each and every one of them had been saddled and bridled, they would have forgotten their prior existence and would be champing at their bits in anticipation of a damn good gallop northwards.

Neptune, although pleased with the business of turning back time and the evacuation of the many tourists, had to concede that it was a bit of a hit and miss to say the least. He looked around now at the centaurs as they grouped together and sympathised with them in their consternation. Half-man,

156

half-horse obviously didn't appeal to any of them. It didn't appeal much to him either, but too late to fix it now. Anyway, they too would forget their former existence any moment now.

After all, he considered, he was only god of the seas, horses and earthquakes and really, all in, it was quite remarkable what he had achieved thus far. For the descendents of the gods were not working on full godly powers as yet and it had been rather dangerous using them as conductors like that. Shaking his head, he admonished himself, why it could have killed them, indeed wiped them out.

He looked around now at the tourists who had been left behind. It was unfortunate, but they would just have to grin and bear it. At least they had a cup of coffee each. That pleased him no end, for it had been just a whim really. No more than a tiny thought that had snuck in there in the heat of meditation. He found it very satisfying that the thought had transferred across into reality, as it opened up a completely new spectrum of ideas to him. It seemed now that anything was possible.

He smiled down at a few hundred tourists who hadn't been caught in his meditative net. He was still trying to work out why they didn't go with the others. Indeed, what were they up at the time of transposition. He sniffed suspiciously. Drugs. That was it. He could damn well smell drugs. All of them sat there on the grass collectively staring in an open-mouthed manner at the centaurs and at Neptune, as their coffee spilled into their laps. He was about to administer a damn good finger wagging "now see what happens when you ..." lecture when the thunder of horses' hooves came their way.

Neptune turned to watch them approach and he swelled with pride as the horses galloped past in their seemingly endless line. Yes, quite an accomplishment, he congratulated himself again. The centaurs had at last forgotten who they once were and Neptune watched, as with their bows and arrows strapped over their backs they joined the riders, keeping pace with the best of them.

He turned then and smiled at the tourists.

"Well must dash you bad things, I have a war to run. Yes, indeed, it's time to kick ass."

His audience stared back with eyes as wide as saucers and on many a chin drool trickled down. Others who had found it all entirely too much, were stretched out in a dead faint. With a final wave, Neptune disappeared to the acoustics of approximately three hundred coffee cups crashing to the ground.

Sarah Scott

Wound

I learned of it later
much later
after you were gone
and I opened one of your books in the store
casually
and found littered carelessly, thoughtlessly, in the pages
stolen fragments of myself.

Immortal

Fighting the drone of attempted education
A languid finger traces the names
Of those who have passed before
And sought to immortalise themselves in wood.
Meaningless now,
I wonder who they were
As I idly add myself to their ranks

Sweep

Time measured in five-minute intervals
That last for years.
Each sweep of the second hand
Subdues my spirit
Dulls my mind
Bleeds my soul.

After the Funeral

Dust dances across the floor
As you walk in.
Books, boxes, chairs,
Piled in forgotten heaps.
This is where she lived
And died.
The woman you never knew.
Were you hoping to find some clue here?
Do you think you can know her from what
she left behind?
Or are you simply searching for yourself?

Pygmalion

All she could really remember were his hands. She believed that was what she had first fallen in love with. They were stained grey from the clay that he had been working with, and moving with such careful deliberation, shaping and moulding the material under them. She had watched him, utterly fascinated by the sculpture taking shape under his hands, by seeing it come to life. So fascinated that she had missed two classes and half of lunch before he was finished and she was able to tear her gaze away.

He had a scar on the middle finger of his left hand. The pinkish skin was smooth under her finger tips, but his palms were rougher from work, he had told her when she'd pressed her own to his just to see how much bigger his hand was than hers, and he'd curled his fingers, easily engulfing hers. She thought it was a promise of protection.

His fingers were used to shaping curves and angles, so it came as no surprise that they slid so easily along the planes of her tear stained cheeks, gathering drops of salt water as if they were something infinitely more precious, barely glancing over the bruises on her face. The sound of his fist thumping against clay echoed in her head from the depths of memory. It didn't sound all that different from fist against flesh, and not all of sculpting was a gentle process. He smoothed her hair back, before roughened palms moved over her bare arms and his hand engulfed hers, lying limp by her sides. A statement of possession.

Missing in Action

Next to the roses
The little star he crafted was lost.
For a long time she forgot it was there.
Remembrance coming
with the death of flowers, and the fading
Of that other love

William Purcell

Running in Square Circles

Premature retirement is a soul-destroying thing. One minute you're working away, studying and chasing promotion, next some stupid pratt decides to store two gallons of petrol under the sink then sets the chip pan on fire. By the time we arrived it had all cooked itself up really nicely and as I went through the front door the petrol can decided to let go. I left via the front door wearing the kitchen door, about two feet off the ground and rising. My mates told me later I was quite impressive, doing triple sulkas and back flips before hitting the wall. Anyway, one year and a bit later I was retired, bored and on the verge of succumbing to Australian soap operas.

Then I saw the article in the paper about the old maze at Kilmurny House, reputedly the biggest and oldest maze in the country. Following the purchase of the estate by the National Trust it was to be opened to the public. It seemed a nice way to pass the day, so I jumped into the car and set off.

It was a warm sunny autumn day, what Gran used to call an Indian summer and at one point I stopped, put the roof of the car down and considered just driving. I decided to go with the original plan though and arrived at Kilmurny just after twelve. The sun was high and hot so I slightly selfconsiously jammed a baseball cap on my head and went to find the maze.

Several signposts later I saw it and was suitably impressed. Ancient beech hedges that were all of nine foot tall and a foot thick stood in glorious golds and yellows, planted and trimmed to form a maze over a century ago.

Paying my £2.50 I passed through the turnstile and entered the short avenue that led to the maze proper. I decided to use the technique used in my time as a fireman, choose a side and keep your hand on that wall. I chose the left, that meant I would keep my left hand in contact with the hedges on my left, then to exit, turn and place my right hand on the hedge. If I didn't change or try to skip areas I should eventually get to the centre without getting lost. Once or twice as I passed others I received a few strange looks as I walked into obvious dead ends, around the sides and back out again. At first I was slightly embarrassed but it soon became amusing and I began to exaggerate my movements just to watch the reaction. Two small boys and a girl began to follow me.

"Hey mister, what the hell ur ye daen?"

I tried to explain as simply as possible.

"Dis it work?"

I assured them it did.

The girl, who looked about five or six, stared at me around a lollipop in that all knowing, disconcerting way that only a child can.

"I want to follow him." she announced.

The eldest boy, around nine, looked from her to me.

"Wid ye mind?"

"Well, what about your parents?" I asked, in a vain attempt to say no.

"Ma maw's in the hoose." said the bigger boy.

"An wur faithers at work. He's a security man an wears a uniform." continued the smaller.

"An we're here by wurselves." finished his brother.

"I like you." pronounced the girl.

Mentally I submitted. "Ok come along, but you must do what I tell you?"

The little girl nodded sagely, dislodging a large dribble of lolly juice from her chin which soaked into the front of her already damp dress.

"Right then, let's go then. Left hand on the hedge and don't skip corners."

"Whit's yer name mister?" asked the younger boy

"Charlie. What's yours?"

Ah'm Andy. Ma big brothers Davey an ma wee sisters Anastasia. Ma maw ca's her wee princess."

"Wee pest mair like it." said the one I now knew as Davey.

There didn't seem to be an answer to that so I reached out my left hand, touched the hedge and started walking. The children duly followed my example and for the next ten minutes or so we walked on, sometimes me in front other times the kids. My right hand became sticky with lolly juice as Anastasia decided occasionally to hold my free hand.

The kids chattered on about everything and nothing until we finally reached the centre. There were a couple of benches and a plaque that told a bit about the history of the house and the maze. Anastasia, I thought it a rather grand name for the sticky precocious child who seemed hell bent on getting me as sticky as her, announced that she needed the toilet. Davey and Andy watched for my reaction.

168

"I, I don't think there are toilets in here, can you wait till we get back out again?"

She shook her head slowly, staring at me with large sombre eyes.

"Jist dae whit ye usually dae." said Davey.

"But the man might mind." she replied.

Desperate for a way out but terrified at the thought of what was the usual way I mumbled my agreement. "Yes, just do what you usually do."

She held the lollipop out to me. "Please would you hold this for me, they two wid jist eat it."

Gingerly I took the lolly from her and she skipped round the corner of the maze. As we awaited her return I studied it pondering how many germs must exist on it's sticky surface and if I could steal it and sell it to Porton Down as some form of biological weapon.

"This is the first time we've ever got tae the middle." announced Davey "Usually we jist wander aboot an then go back oot."

"Aye, an now we know how tae dae it we kin offer tae be guides tae people, maybe earn some dosh." Andy looked smug.

My nose tickled at the smell of smoke, someone was burning leaves or garden rubbish.

"How much dae ye think we could charge tae rescue people who goat lost mister?" Andy asked.

"What?"

"Ye know, we could be the maze rescue service an when people goat lost they wid pay us tae get them oot."

"I don't really know, I suppose you could haggle over the price, that way the more desperate they were the more the would be willing to pay."

"Aye, that sounds good. Whit's haggle?"

"Well you kind of argue about the price till you're both happy."

The two boys sat and thought about it. I realised that the lolly was resting against my shirt. My thoughts about how to clean it were broken by someone shouting about getting water. There was an unsettling edge to the voice. Standing I looked around, there wasn't much to see except the tall hedges and a patch of blue sky above them. Still, something, call it instinct or whatever said it was time to leave.

"Where's Anastasia?"

"Huvin a pee." answered Davey.

"Or maybe a shite, she's takin a long time." added his brother.

Or maybe she's got herself lost I thought.

"Anastasia." I shouted, but there was no immediate response. I called again, still no answer. I was about to call again when I heard more raised voices. There was a definite note of panic and I strained to hear what they were saying. A knot formed in my stomach as I picked out a few and slowly realised what was happening. The maze was on fire.

"Right boy's, it's time we were going, Anastasia, where are you?"

I strode over to the corner where she had disappeared, my heart sinking as an empty stretch of maze was revealed. My body shuddered as a deep chill swept through it.

"Right boys, come this way, quickly, Anastasia's got lost."

"Trust her," muttered Andy, ambling slowly over.

"Come on. We have to find her." I started down the maze, followed the corner to the left, still no sign of her. I walked quickly to the end. It was a 'T' junction and it was empty in both directions. Which way? Frustration turned to anger as the two boys slowly turned the corner behind me.

"Anastasia!" No answer "Anastasia! Where are you?" Still nothing. I turned and shouted at the boys. "Right you two, get your arses down here and wait at this corner. Don't move away from it."

"Whit's bitin' you?" asked Davey. "She'll no be far an she's no likely tae die before she gets oot. She's got hersel lost in here a couple o' times before."

I waited till they were closer. "Look, I don't want to panic you but can you smell that smoke?"

"Aye. So?

"Well there's a fire out there and I want to get out of here just in case it spreads to this bloody maze."

"Well that'll no be a problem, aw we need tae dae is go back tae the centre an stick oot wur right hauns an we'll be oot in nae time."

Totally lost at this onslaught of logic I raised my hands in submission. "Look, just humour me. Stand here till I check round here." I half walked half ran to the next corner. It led to a short passage with another 'T' junction and was empty. A few

170

steps and a glance left and right failed to produce Anastasia. Resisting the temptation to go further, I returned to the boys.

"Give me a minute till I check out this side." I growled as I passed them. Turning the corner, I was met by the crouching figure of Anastasia and a familiar odour.

"It's rude to watch!" she snapped, pulling her dress close.

I turned quickly, apologising, cleared my throat and asked if she would be much longer.

"It's no ma fault if Ah'm constipated. Ah'll no be a minute. Wid ye mind waitin roon the corner."

Without thinking I complied with her wishes and waved the boys towards me. As I awaited further developments on Anastasia's constipation I looked at the sky, clouds of dirty yellowish white smoke were starting to obscure the sun. Andy followed my gaze then back to me with questions filling his eyes. Before he could ask Anastasia appeared pulling at her knickers.

She opened her mouth to speak but, more intent on getting us out of the maze I stopped her with a wave of my hand. "Right let's move." I turned away from where the smoke was rising and ushered the children in front of me. "Quickly now, we'll need to hurry, it's getting late and I, I." God, what could I say. "I've got to get home soon."

Andy looked at me, one eyebrow raised. "Ah thoght ye said ye'd aw day?"

"Did I? I must have forgot." I looked ahead. The choice was left or right. Which way? Wait till we reach it, both ways looked the same, "This way, I ushered the children left and moved in front of them trying to see which way the path turned. Relief at the sight of a right turn was short lived as a dead end appeared as I rounded the corner.

"Shit, c'mon, back the other way." we turned and began to go back.

"How dae we no dae the haun thing?" asked Davie.

"This will show you how easy it is to get lost if you don't." I replied, hoping he wouldn't question me further.

The path turned left then right to another junction. Davie reached it first, looked both ways then recoiled back, crashing into his brother and knocking him to the ground. He turned to me, eyes wide, mouth open. I reached the corner and looked round. At the end of a long stretch of path the hedges were burning, flames leaping from the dry leaves and branches to join an ever-increasing pall of white smoke. There was no hiding it from them now. Anastasia screamed and fell.

I grabbed Andy's arm and pulled him to his feet, pushing him away from the fire, telling Davie to follow him. I picked up Anastasia, holding her against my chest and ran after them. For a few minutes we ran without thinking, turning this way and that until we came to another dead end.

"We'll have to go back, find another way."

"But the fires back that way!" Davy's voice was shaky.

"Well, we can't go this way." I gestured at the hedges in frond and around us. "We'll go back to the last corner and try another way."

Anastasia looked at me, tear tracks leaving two clean lines down her cheeks. "Do what the man says." she said, her eyes never moving from mine.

We set off again, always trying to head away from the fire, but again, having run along another long passage found ourselves in another dead end. But this time there was no going back, smoke and a hint of flame showed through the hedge behind us. The children's rising panic began to infect me as I lowered Anastasia and sank to a crouch. "Shit, shit, shit." I swore.

"I'm sorry, but there was no paper." Anastasia said, fiddling with the front of her dress.

I stared at her, at a loss to comprehend what she was saying. "What?"

"There was no paper. You're sleeve" She looked at the ground.

"That's OK" I said while trying to think. If we couldn't go back we had to go forward. I got up and started to pull wildly at the branches that blocked our way, but the hedges were old and thick and surprisingly strong. After a few minutes I began to slow. I forced myself to think. I stopped and stared back, looking at the fire behind us. Closing my eyes I took some deep breaths, exhaling slowly, forcing myself to be calm, listening to the shouts from outside. What if nobody knew we were there? Surely they would, I had paid to get in, but what if they didn't count people in and out. And the children hadn't paid!

"Right," I said, "here's the plan. I'm going to make a hole in the hedge, Anastasia, you watch the fire back there and let me know when it gets worse, boys, I want you to shout

'Help' as loudly as you can." I felt more in control again and resumed my attack on the hedge, but this time with a bit more thought.

"It's getting through the other hedge." said Anastasia, pulling at my shirt. I looked back, flames had broken through and were spreading along the surface of the hedges towards us. I stepped up my attack on the branches in front, just a little more. My fingers were starting to bleed and scratches covered my arms, But I ignored them. If I could just get the thicker branch out of the way there would be enough room to get through. Angrily I began to kick at it and slowly it began to give way. A glance back showed time was getting short, the boys shouts had died and the three kids looked alternately at me then at the approaching fire.

From somewhere to the left and behind us a high-pitched scream began and seemed as if it would never stop. When it did it was only for a moment and it began again, and again.

"Whit's that?" asked Davie.

"Somebody doing what you're supposed to be doing, screaming to attract attention! Now get shouting, the pair of you. Shout so loud that I can't hear them"

I hoped they believed me, I had heard fear like that in screams before and fire is one of the most fearful things that there is. Someone was in a worse state than we were. Stepping back I drop kicked the branch. It gave with a loud crack and we had our hole.

I pushed through with difficulty and turned to help the kids. The fire had covered about half the length of the passage we were leaving and the smoke had began to reach us. *'Just in time.'* I thought then turned to see where we were now. To the left was a dead end and to the right the passage turned back toward the fire. I ran to the corner and looked round, it was almost as long as the one we had left and already smoke was pouring through at the far end. I felt ready to give up but another bout of screaming began and I determined that wasn't going to happen to us.

"Wait here." I told the children. I ran to the burning end of the passage and looked round, I almost cheered as it doubled back the way I had come, away from the fire. I called the children but after a few steps they stopped, unsure. I ran back and, picking up Anastasia, told the boys to hold on to me and not to let go. In a tight huddle we scurried along the passage and as we reached the corner another scream began, but this time it was closer, and getting nearer. I almost stopped but the boys kept me going and we rounded the corner and once more were heading away from the fire.

Then I did stop, as something crashed against the hedge at our back and the scream stopped.

"Go to the end of this passage, no further." I told the kids and turned back toward the fire.

The hedge thrashed about as I approached and I could hear someone moaning. Peering through the smoke I made my way closer. A hand pushed through, blistered and bleeding, the fingers stretching out as if to find a haven. I instinctively reached for it but another scream, so close it was almost inside my head, stopped me. I stepped back, feeling small and helpless. I wanted to reach out, grip that hand and pull whoever it was through to safety but I knew it was impossible. I backed away, afraid to make a sound and as tears of frustration and uselessness began to flow, I turned and ran back to the children.

Luck seemed to be with us and we managed to move further ahead of the fire before we were blocked again. Hope slipped a little and despair crept closer. I started shouting and began kicking at the hedge with the sole of my shoe. The children watched me, fear etched in their faces. I was unsure if it was fear of the fire or the lunatic beside them. A branch gave beneath my onslaught and my foot pushed on through the hedge. Searing pain paralysed me as the broken branch sank deep into my calf muscle and I screamed as I have never screamed before. And when I finished that scream I screamed again. When I finished that a familiar sound reached us, two-tone horns, but was it the Fire Brigade or the police, and what could they do when they got here?

My leg was still through the hedge and part of the hedge was through my leg. Gritting my teeth I pulled back, imagination creating the sound of sucking as the branch pulled free. The horns were much closer now and I heard the deep rumble of a big diesel in low gear. Hope rose again then fell with me as I put weight on my injured leg which promptly collapsed. The world went grey and began to spin. I threw up and passed out.

I came to with Anastasia shaking me, pleading with me to wake up. Davey was tying the remnants of his shirt round my leg. A loudspeaker crackled and a voice asked if there was anyone in the maze and would they make their presence known. It sounded so formal that it was almost laughable. Together we shouted and waited for an answer. Nothing! Again we shouted. This time a voice answered asking where we were.

As soon as I shouted "Here!" I felt stupid. At least the other person had the decency not to shout 'Where' back, instead he asked if there was someway we could show our position. I took off what was left of my shirt and tried to wave it above the hedge but couldn't get high enough. Andy asked if I would lift him up and he would wave it. I tried to lift him but the pain in my leg caused me to put him down before I fell. I turned and leant against the hedge, closing my eyes in frustration. Anastasia tugged my hand.

"I could climb up you if you stay like that. I'm the lightest and I do it with my Dad sometimes."

"Ok I'll try."

The boys helped her up and soon she was standing on my shoulders. With each wave a flare of pain swept through me. My head began to swim.

"Over there!" came a voice from far, far away as my leg gave way and I slid to the ground. All we could do now was wait.

I looked up as, with a metallic clatter, the end of a ladder appeared over us, stretched out over the tops of the hedges, followed a few moments later by a fireman with a shorter ladder which he lowered down beside us.

Soon we were outside the maze, safe in the back of an ambulance where a medic was cleaning and dressing my leg. The children sat opposite me, each with a drink, watching as I was treated.

Davey said to no one in particular, "Well that's pit a stop tae that plan."

"What plan?" I asked

"Tae make money by bein guides in the maze." He stared at his drink.

A policeman stuck his head inside the ambulance, "Right kids, let's get you home."

"In a Police car?" asked Anastasia.

"Yes" replied the officer.

"Maw willnae like that," she said seriously, "She'll go on aboot whit the neighbours think."

They rose to leave but Anastasia paused at the door and turned back to me. "Here, whit did ye dae wi ma lollipop?"

The pub had been there for almost two hundred years.

It stood far enough from the Broomielaw far a sailor to feel he had left his ship behind, but close enough for him to stagger easily to his berth when he had drunk his fill.

Into its dim interior walked Michael Paul. His appearance caused little comment among the few present as he ordered a pint of heavy. A drink almost forgotten behind a screen of cocktails and designer beers.

As he waited he looked around, The pub's interior mirrored to an extent the shabby exterior but it was a warm comfortable shabbiness. Dark varnished wood dominated the decor with that deep glow that is only achieved by age, smooth brass complemented it.

An old man stood almost directly opposite him staring into space, his heavy overcoat and cap at odds with the mild weather outside. He stood in a narrow gap between the wall and a round roughly plastered pillar. Michael nodded to him but either the man did not notice the gesture or ignored it. Behind him three men sat at a table discussing the contents of a newspaper spread in front of them. His drink arrived and his thoughts turned inward as he slowly sipped at it.

"Hey, any chance o' some service?" Michael started at the sudden voice. As he waited for the barman the owner of the voice turned to Michael.

"Howzit gaun Big Man?"

It took a few seconds for Michael to realise that the man was talking to him.

"Eh? Not bad, could be better. But, what's the point of complaining."

"Not a lot, but sometimes jist gettin it aff yer chest can help. Hey, if you could drag yer arse aff that seat ye could gie's three hauf pints o' light." The barman rose and busied himself with the order.

Yes changed to "Aye" as Michael answered, the man's accent stirring the memory of a language he hadn't used in a long time.

"Aye." he repeated, savouring the sound.

The other looked at him and smiled in response, "See. ye've got a smile on yer face already. Dae ye fancy a game o'

Doms?"

"Doms?"

"Dominoes. Ye ken, wee black things wi' spots. We play fur hauf pints. Ma name's Dan by the way"

Michael thought for a second.

"Aye. Though I'm not very good."

The other laughed. "Ach, they a' say that, c'mon." He paid for his drinks, picked them up and made for the table, Michael following. He was one of the three who had been reading the paper.

"He's Jimmy, the baldy wan's Gordon." Said Dan as he sat down.

"Hi, my name's Michael."

Dominoes were spilled across the table and stirred, each made their selection and the game began. All to soon Michael made a mistake, forced his partner to chap and the game was lost.

"Well at least yer honest Mick. ye did say ye wurny much good."

"I didn't think I was that bad, but I'll tell you what, I'll buy the drinks till we win a game."

"Suits me fine, shuffle them then."

The Dominoes were stirred, another game played, Michael bought the half pints again. And again. Eventually he won and his delight at slamming down the final Domino made the barman look toward the table. His glee knew no bounds and he offered to buy the drinks again.

"No bloody likely," snorted Dan, "they two's been drinkin' free on you a' night."

The half pint he received as his prize tasted better than all the fancy drinks he had ever consumed.

"Are ye workin'?"

"You could say that."

"Ah suppose that means aye.' muttered Gordon. "Whit dae ye dae?"

"I'm a professional liar I suppose."

The other three stared at him, consternation on their faces.

Michael smiled at their reaction.

"Fur the luv o' God. whit the hell diz that mean."

"Well. I'm in advertising, got my own agency."

"Ye don't seem awfae pleased aboot it." said Dan sitting

back in his seat. "Personally speakin'. Ah find it a novelty talkin' tae somebody wi' a job."

Afraid that he might spoil his newfound friendship Michael explained that an ability as an artist combined with a vivid imagination had given him a career that had eventually led to a successful business. He then continued, the open handed honesty of the three men and the effect of the few drinks allowing him to speak more openly than he had done for years. It had all seemed too easy. He had never felt the sweat of hard labour. never tried to ease overstrained muscles into a less painful position, and it jarred with the memory of his father collapsing exhausted into his chair after a long days work.

"Ye're fuckin daft!"

Dan's comment put a lid on what he realised was a well of self pity.

Michael felt better.

Much later he walked a little unsteadily home. The couple he met at the entrance to the flats looked at him dubiously.

"Been playin' Doms." Michael muttered as he fumbled for his keys and began to climb the stairs. As an excuse it only attracted stranger looks and heads shaken behind his back.

That night he was asleep almost instantly.

The headache he felt the next morning was not a new experience, but coupled with the memory of the previous night made him reach for the phone and tell the office he was having a few days off. He had some life to catch up on. Those days were spent revisiting the city he had grown up in.

It was a time of mixed emotions. Joy at seeing places he had never visited. Sorrow at the supermarket that sprawled where he had lived as a child. But no matter how the day went the highlight was always the visit to the pub for a blether about nothing and a few hands of Doms.

It was one of these nights he first spoke with Auld Eck. the old man he had noticed when he had first came into the pub. He had since agreed with the majority that the Auld Eck was daft, senile or both. He always stood in the same place, drinking long, slow half pints. He would lean against the pillar alternately muttering to himself or staring vacantly at the bar. Michael had watched him, wondering what he was thinking, but soon regarded him as part of the decor.

That night Michael was earlier than usual and he began

to look at the pictures of sailing ships that were scattered around the walls. He was attracted to one of a green hulled clipper with all sails set and murmured his disappointment when he saw it was unnamed.

"Thermopolae."

Michael turned to see who had spoken. Auld Eck was looking at him. "The ship's the 'Thermopolae', named efter the pass where 300 Spartans held aff the Persian Army."

Michael stared at the old man. Gone was the vacant expression.

"Was that the fastest clipper?"

Eck stepped back from the bar and leant against the pillar, closed his eyes and seemed to think for a minute.

"Well, that's a matter of opinion. The 'Champion of the Seas' made the longest run in 24 hours, but the 'Cutty Sark' and the 'Thermopolae' were reckoned to be the best. Which wan o' them wis best wis never proved 'cos they never raced directly agin each ither." His eyes seemed to brighten. "Except wance, They left Hangkow on the same tide, it seemed the hale world wis watchin' us. Ghostin doon the South China sea wi studdin' sails set, We even spread hammocks frae the yards tae try an squeeze the last ounce a' power frae the breeze."

Michael stood entranced as the story unfolded, how the two ships had separated as each Captain had tried to win some slight advantage then disaster as the 'Cutty Sark' lost her rudder in the Indian Ocean. not once, but twice, losing four days sailing. Eventually she berthed in London Docks but only one day behind her great rival.

"They said it wis inconclusive but tae me the 'Cutty Sark' wis fastest. efter a', she wis Clyde built." Auld Eck stopped talking and turned back to the bar as the brightness faded from his eyes. Michael stood, puzzled by the sudden change.

Dan's voice broke into his thoughts, inviting him to a game of cribbage. Michael played badly, something gnawing at him, taking the edge from his concentration.

"Wiz that daft auld bugger annoying you?" asked Dan as he pegged another two holes.

"No, not really, it was interesting listening to him."

"Aye, when he tells a story he can fair get a grip on ye. He wis tellin me aboot the shipyairds an buildin' the 'Queen Mary'. Ye feel ye're there."

The conversation stopped and the game of cribbage was

abandoned as Gordon and Jimmy arrived and the never ending Domino challenge resumed. His previous uneasiness vanished in the banter.

Michael finished his self granted holiday and threw himself back into his business but always kept a couple of nights free to visit the pub and his new friends.

Several times in the following year he heard Auld Eck tell stories of past events, always with the same vivid detail and each time Michael felt the same something nagging away at the back of his mind but he never resolved it.

On the 13th July Michael's company won a major contract and by four o'clock everything was signed. A champagne party began and just after eleven he was dropped off, slightly drunk, outside his flat. Once inside he made a coffee, slumped onto the sofa and used the remote to switch on the T.V. A picture of a full rigged ship moving down a river flickered onto the screen. Tiny figures scampered among the rigging and masts. Micheal sat upright, suddenly sober. Auld Eck! When he told a story it was always in great detail, accurate, and in the first person, as if he had been there.

The coffee was left as he pulled on his jacket and made for the pub. When he reached it time had been called and people were leaving. Auld Eck's corner was empty.

The barman asked if he wanted a quick one. Michael declined and left. He had wanted to ask Eck about his stories. where he got them from, how he could know so much detail.

He was almost home when his name was called. Looking round he saw Eck sprawled in a close mouth and hurried over.

"What's the matter? Are you alright?" he asked, raising the old man into a sitting position.

"Ah'm feenished son. Gonnae somethin' fur me, eh."

"You're alright, don't move. I'll phone an ambulance."

"Naw, wait."

Michael held up his hand to stop him talking. "No, you wait, I'll get an ambulance, you'll be fine. Don't worry."

"Ah'm no worried."

"Oh shut up Eck, just lie still."

Michael stared up and down the street. Where was a phone? The empty street offered no immediate help. Eck's hand gripped his jacket.

"Settle doon son, Ah'm done an' neither you or a fleet a'

ambulances'll change it. But Ah wis lookin' fur you, you've got it. You're aware. Jist tell the pillar Ah'll no be back, eh." Michael held his hand till its grip on his jacket loosened.

Eck lay still, a smile on his face.

Micheal called out till someone answered and promised to get an ambulance. He sat there cradling the old man, unaware of the gathering crowd or that he was weeping until a Police car arrived. Later, when Eck had been taken away and he had answered some questions he returned home and went to bed. He slept fitfully, Eck's last words bouncing around in his head.

It was a few days before he returned to the pub. Gordon was alone and greeted him with the news of Eck's death.

"Aye, Ah know, it's a shame," responded Micheal as he leant on the bar waiting for service. "dae ye want a pint?"

Naw, Ah've tae sign oan in hauf an hour. Better no be late."

Soon he was alone with his thoughts and came to decision. When the barman went into the cellar he walked round and stood in Auld Eck's space. Self consciously he turned and whispered to it. "Auld Eck won't be back, he asked me to tell you."

"We know." said a voice in his head, "he's with us now."

Micheal stiffened.

"Don't worry, he's happy with us and we have so much to tell you."

Michael stood as the spirits of seamen, shipyard workers and others who had drank in the pub in years gone by told their stories.

Dan, Gordon and Jimmy eventually tired of approaching him and being rebuffed and left him to himself. Michael became a constant presence in the pub, standing in the space between the pillar and the wall. Newcomers to the pub would comment on the young man in the shabby, but once expensive clothes who stood with a never ending half pint staring into nothingness and occasionally muttering to himself.

Jack Hastie

Samhain. (All Hallows` Eve.)

Tonight
all graves gape
all urns open
all requiems are unsaid.

The Eve of All Saints
is all evils` eve
and permits the return of the dead
from darkness
curling into light
between suns
in the brightness of night.

Till dawn
like a gong
summons the shades
to their ashes and graves
and like lead
seals them from sight.

Winter Evening Walk

What am I trying to do –
solve the jigsaw puzzles
of the constellations?

Track the planets as they glide
like chess-men
among the thin stars?

Shout "check"
when Mars or Jupiter
ghosts into Taurus
slap on top of Aldebaran?

Or "mate"
when the Evening Star
laughs above the sickle
of the cowering low moon?

What am I thinking of –
pawing the stars into meanings?
Nosing after comets and meteor showers
like a fox hunting rabbits?

As cataracts cloud the eye
the aurora casts curtains
across the blind night
veiling the precession of the equinoxes
from my understanding.

I give up.
Kick a stone for my dog to chase.

Resurrection

Get pissed on a daft Friday evening
in the Clachaig or the Kingshouse.

Put up a tent in the peat
by Jacksonville
or doss in Downie`s Barn
under an old overcoat
without benefit of air bed or sleeping bag.

Pump up a brass primus
and fork baked beans round a mess tin.

Saturday morning –
austere blue spaces
emptying below my heels
on the Rannoch Wall
or sweeping to infinity
from the saw-sharp cat walk
of the Aonach Eagach.

Once
in blind silver mist
that stung like aftershave
cutting love bites
in the beautiful, milk smooth throat
of Twisting Gully.

These were my ultimate places
ladders to Paradise.
Get buried on a dirty Sunday night
down the brutal, gridlocked Lochside road.

Monday morning –
numb awakening
to the grotesque, Hieronymus Bosch world
of Midden Street Junior Secondary
presided over by an –
understandably –
alcoholic headmaster.

Every good Friday
a resurrection.

The summits and the routes
were like spirits
and I stepped among them
as an equal
like a risen god.

Dialing God

I read in the news recently that somebody had been plagued by unwanted telephone calls because his number was very similar to that of God, as quoted in a recently released film. I checked out the number and dialled it.

"Thank you for calling God," said a cool, sexy recorded female voice. "To help us improve our service we may record or monitor your call. Please choose one of the following options. If you want to speak to Jesus, press 1. If you want to talk to Allah, press 2. If you want to talk to Rama, press 3. If you want to talk to Buddha, press 4. For any other god or goddess, press 5."

Resisting the temptation to dally with laughter loving Aphrodite or perhaps share a drunken joke with Bacchus, I pressed 1.

"In order that we can process your request more effectively," continued the voice, "please select one of the following options. If you want to save a loved one from terminal illness, press 1. If you want to get rich quick, press 2. If you want to be lucky in love, press 3. For a statement of the current balance of your unconfessed mortal sin, press 4. For all other services, press 5."

I pressed 5.

"Please key in your six digit pass code. This is your date of birth unless you have changed it, followed by # and then your seven character post code."

I complied.

"Thank you. For security purposes please key in the first and third characters of your mother's maiden name."

I did.

"Thank you. Please hold the line. One of our advisers will attend to you as soon as possible."

Then the Hallelujah Chorus came on line. At the end of each rendering of the finale the voice interrupted, "Thank you for being patient. Your call is in a queue. You will be attended to as soon as one of our advisers is available."

At last the heavenly music cut; the phone crackled.

"Mr Hastie," said a male voice with an Asian accent, "this is Customer Services. Archangel Gabriel speaking. How may I help you?"

"I want to speak to Jesus," I said.

"He's on the other line just now, but if you'd like to speak to one of his senior personal aides, I'll transfer the call."

There was a click; then the cool recorded voice took over again. "If you want to speak to the Pope, press 1. If you want to speak to the Reverend Ian Paisley press 2 If you want to speak to George W. Bush, press 3. If you want to speak to Tony Blair, press 4. If you want to speak to Nicky Gumbell, press 5 To return to the main menu press * 0."

As there were no other options I chose 4.

The Hallelujah Chorus resumed, interrupted only by regular assurances that " your call is important to us and will be answered as soon as possible." I was reflecting that, had my request been to save a dear one from terminal illness, I might be too late, when the receiver crackled into life again.

"Hi, Jack. Tony here. Sorry about the delay, but we've managed to get waiting times down below what they were under the Tories. What's your problem?"

"I wanna get published," I whinged.

"Right. I think I see where your coming from. Now I'm a fairly straight sort of guy, so I'm going to ask you to trust me. Saddam *did* have weapons of mass destruction and he and Gordon were within forty five minutes of using them to sabotage my bid to bring Britain into the Euro and become the first president of the European Union. By the way John Prescott's a fairly straight sort of guy too, and I never sold peerages and Patricia and Charles are doing a great job and..."

"Hold on," I interrupted. "I just wanna get published. Wondered if Jesus might see his way to work a wee miracle. Something like the water-into-wine trick he pulled at Cana. Turn the crap I write into something publishable."

The line crackled. "Oh!" Tony seemed startled. "I think you'll have to speak to him personally about that. I'll transfer the call."

There was another blast of Hallelujah. Then the familiar, "Thank you for calling God. If you want to speak to Jesus, press 1."

I gave up.

Self Portrait

Yet again
I lean forward to adore my Narcissus face.

I've adjusted this composition many times
to find the perfect balance
and to emphasise the symbolism
and I think the final effect is striking.

Take the background;
to the right
steep, pine-furred slopes sweep to an ice-clad peak
precisely placed
to fit the proportions of the golden mean.
That's for Eternity.

The gibbous moon
balancing high on the left
signifies Time.

But I still have one problem –
how am I to depict Change?

With a torn fingernail
I scribble the surface.
Instantly my face wrinkles
into age.

Horrified, I step back
and hurl a time-stone.
The glass moment shatters.

Gradually the loch's eye focuses again
and the images return –
Time and Eternity.
But my face is gone.

Outsider

I roll out my sleeping bag
pillowed by pine needles
across fox-watched trails
on this forest floor.

A boulder field below
blear the anxious Argus eyes
of human hives in rows
geometrical.

Here
among the bowels of the trees
stenched by foxes
I stretch out and sleep
under the tongue of the glacier.
Dream of to-morrow's sword play.

Behind those anxious eyes,
double glazed against pine spores,
Airwick and Persil
mask fox reek.
Plastic cups measure souls.

To-morrow
I'll lace my boots and go
past waterfalls and thunder
by mountainsides and stars
up to the heat of the ice.

Cast my sword across the summit.
Lair with foxes.

The next morning
I will shower and shave
put on a tie.
Strangle through veils of Airwick
into a pure land
fox-sterile
Persil white.
Robe myself in plastic.

The Wall

It was a huge wall, built of great stones that dripped with moss. An ancient grey, slimy wall that leaned out over the road as if it was sick and might soon collapse and die.

What lay behind it was a mystery.

Every day Mark and Daniel and Sam walked past it on their way to school. And every day they asked themselves the same question; "What is behind this wall?"

One day Mark asked his Papa, "What is behind that wall?"

Papa turned pale and licked his lips nervously. "I wouldn't go near it if I were you. There are two swords, life size carved in stone built into it and below them a dog's tombstone with the inscription, KHAN, AFGHAN HOUND. Born 8th January 1957. Died 15th September 1965.Now why should anyone build a dog's tombstone into a wall?"

"Perhaps that's where the dog died," suggested Daniel.

"Who put the swords there?" asked Mark.

"I have no idea," answered Papa, "but I think something terrible, far too terrible for words.." he broke off.

"What? What?" asked Mark and Daniel together.

"I don't know," admitted Papa. "But promise me you won't ever touch that terrible wall."

A few days later Daniel had a dream. He was walking close to the wall all by himself, on his way back from school. Slowly he became aware of a faint whispering that seemed to be coming from the other side. At first it sounded like the rustling of leaves in the wind, but as Daniel listened the rustling became more and more like a child's voice. It was very soft and indistinct and it was a long time before Daniel could make out any definite words.

But eventually he thought he heard it say, "Help me Daniel. I am a prisoner here. Please help me to escape. Please. Please."

Then Daniel woke up.

The next morning, on the way to school, he told his dream to Mark and Sam.

"Load of rubbish," sneered Sam.

"Was it a boy or a girl?" asked Mark.

"Don't know."

"Did it have a name?"

"I didn't ask."

"I would have asked," insisted Mark. "You'll have to ask if you have the same dream again."

"I don't want to have the dream again," said Daniel. "It was scary."

Daniel didn't have the dream again, but Mark did.

One moment he was in his bed with Tigh, his dog, snuggled up beside him. The next he was walking past the wall, just like Daniel had been. And just like Daniel he was hearing whispers. Like Daniel, he thought at first that it was just the rustling of leaves in the trees, or perhaps the gurgling of water in the ditch by the roadside. But after a while he was sure that it was the voice of a child whispering, "Mark please, please help me. Daniel, your friend has forsaken me. And cruel Sam just laughed. But you are a kind boy. Please help me to escape from behind this terrible wall."

Even though it was a dream Mark had all his wits about him. He remembered what he had said to Daniel about asking the voice if it had a name.

"Who are you?" he asked.

"A child like you."

"What's your name?"

"Molly," whispered the voice. "You must help me."

"How did you get behind the wall, and what's it like in there?"

"Horrible! Please help me to escape, Mark."

"How am I going to do that?"

"Put your hand into the wall. When it comes right through to the other side I will clasp it in mine and then you must pull me through the wall to freedom. Promise me that you will do that for me."

Mark was just about to promise when Tigh licked him on the nose and wakened him up.

"Bowf," barked Tigh and Mark felt that somehow she knew about his dream and was warning him to have nothing to do with the whisperer in the wall.

The next morning, on the way to school, Mark told Daniel and Sam about his dream and how Tigh had wakened him just as he was about to promise to put his hand into the wall.

"She was warning you," said Daniel solemnly.

Sam laughed out loud. "Yeah, man. That'll be right. A dog that reads dreams! You two are so uncool."

"Right," said Daniel. "You put your hand into the wall, Sam."

"No go," said Sam. "The dream said Mark was to do it. It's all rubbish anyway. It's only a silly old wall."

"Chicken," taunted Daniel.

"If it's only a silly old wall why don't you put your hand into it?" said Mark. "You're always boasting about how great you are, a leader in the Anchor Boys, a striker with Linwood Rangers.

"It's just a wall. It's made of stones. My hand won't go into it."

"Chicken if you don't try," said Daniel.

"No way. It's just stupid dreams."

"Then just do it!" insisted Daniel.

Sam hesitated.

"Chicken. Chicken," chanted Mark and Daniel together.

*****

The three boys waited till Friday after school. They had told no one. Not their mums or dads, schoolteachers or any of their classmates. Mark wanted to tell his Papa, but Sam said he'd only laugh and make a fool of them. And Daniel said that if Mark's Papa knew what they were planning to do he would stop them.

So they kept their plan to themselves and wound their way home from school close to the old moss covered wall. Listening.

Then it started; the whispering.

"Just the wind in the leaves," said Sam.

"There isn't any wind," Daniel pointed out.

"The gurgling of the water in the ditch," said Sam.

Then the whispering thing spoke. "Sam," it said, "Sam. Can you hear me? At last I've found a real boy hero, who will save me from this terrible prison. Are you listening Sam?"

"Aye. Well yes, that's me." Sam was amazed and didn't know what to say.

"Daniel was scared and Mark was chicken," whispered the voice. "Only you are bold enough to rescue poor Molly. You won't fail me, will you?"

"Yes, well no," gurgled Sam.

"I know I can trust you," pleaded Molly.

"It looks like you've got a girl friend," said Mark.

"Don't want a girl friend."

"You mean you're too scared to rescue her," taunted Daniel.

"Tell you what," suggested Mark, "if you pull Molly through the wall she can be Daniel's girl friend.

Sam looked wildly about him.

"You said our dreams were all rubbish," accused Daniel. "Now show us how brave you are."

But Mark was having second thoughts. "Better not," he said. My Papa said the wall was spooky and Tigh stopped me from promising just in time. Don't you touch the wall Sam."

"Spooks aren't real," said Sam. Suddenly all his courage came flooding back. "Spooks are just made up things, like ghosts and witches."

"Then what's behind the wall?" demanded Mark.

"Just an ordinary girl and she's trapped. Somebody must have carried her off and I'm going to rescue her."

He squared his shoulders and stuck his hand into a crevice between two of the biggest stones.

"No!" screamed Mark. But Sam's hand sank smoothly into the depths of the cold grey wall.

"Push your hand through till I can clasp it in mine," whispered Molly. "Further. Further."

Sam gritted his teeth and pushed and slowly his arm began to slide into the wall further and further.

"What's happening?" asked Mark.

"I can feel a hand touching mine, clasping my fingers," said Sam.

"Pull it through," shouted Daniel.

"I can't," gasped Sam. "It's pulling me."

Eyes wide with disbelief Mark and Daniel watched as Sam's arm was drawn slowly into the wall, up to the elbow, up to the armpit.

"Help me," screamed Sam. "Pull me out."

Mark grabbed Sam's other arm and Daniel seized one of his legs, and they both pulled, but remorselessly the wall sucked Sam past his shoulder. Sam put his other foot against the wall and braced himself, but instead of pushing him away his leg began to sink into the stone, up to the ankle, the knee,

195

the thigh. Sam was screaming. His eyes were bulging in terror. Studs of sweat stood on his forehead.

"Don't let me go," he pleaded, but Daniel was forced to drop his leg as Sam's body slid into the wall up to the waist.

Within seconds Sam's other leg had disappeared and the wall slowly oozed like mud in a sucking bog, around his upper body.

As it reached his neck Sam shouted his last frenzied words, "Help me. Don't let go of me." Then the wall was over his mouth and nose. His eyes rolled in a last desperate spasm of terror and then his head was gone and only one arm, with the fingers of the hand clenching and unclenching as they frantically sought for something to hold on to, was left.

"Let his arm go," screamed Daniel. "Don't let his hand grab you or you'll be sucked into the wall too."

Mark released the arm and the boys watched in horror as the cold grey stone inched its way down to the elbow.

"What's going on here?" It was the tall, bearded figure of The Reverend Howel Evans, out walking his dog, who spoke.

"Sam. He's in the wall. There's a thing pulling him in to it," the boys clamoured. "That arm's all that's left of him."

The minister grabbed Sam's wrist as the stone sludged its way across his forearm. The wall spread slowly up to the wrist and then stopped as it came into contact with the Reverend's knuckles.

Howel Evans let go.

The hand flopped. The fingers stopped moving.

The minister said, "I'm afraid he's gone."

The wind ruffled the leaves. Water gurgled in the ditch. The wall was silent as stone. Sam's hand hung limply, like plastic.

George Colkitto

Lost Love

Golden your hair like the sun like the meadow
Why do I stare at each blonde in the street
Cannot compare you would walk like the willow
So futile and fractured is the image I seek
Lost in the crowd I linger on faces
Hoping that someone will smile on me
Love them and kiss them with heart disconnected
I am still tied my spirit consumed

If you are near why do you not touch me
If far away then send me some sign
I knew no fear with you there to hold me
Loneliness empties and terrors confine
Only with you was the world full of wonder
Now it is cold no future of light
I could grow old with only a lost love
To have and to hold In greyness and death
Bring me your lips let me live on your breath

Daffodil

The wind blows cold across the lake
The evening sky is clear and blue
There is no sound not man not beast
The bird sits silent in the tree
And far away a church bell rings
an echo of a time gone by

These are the pictures that I see
in vacant times and pensive mood
They come to haunt that inward eye
that is the curse of solitude
And thus I see that dreams lie still
dead amidst the daffodil

Among the Fields of Barley

For I am
last man standing
Empty be the plane
The sun is high
No shadow falls
No voice across
the barley calls

For I am
last man crying
Icy be the moon
The evening sky
no darkness fears
No wind to rustle
the barley ears

For I am
last man dying
Silent be the breath
The dawn is nigh
No spirits rise
No hand to arc
the barley scythe

18th September 2006

I heard the news today
Four soldiers killed in Afghanistan
No surprise
No shock
Listed in the headlines with Liberal party conference
and football manager sacked
Local casualties unmentioned
Death a statistic

I expected it
Even looked for it as the start for a poem
Am I so distanced from reality
Is compassion so blunted
that seeking to highlight the futility of conflict
I accept and exploit those killed

Today's statement on radio, on television
in tomorrow's newspapers
will be lost in the next attack
Just as those who died last week, last month, last year
those who died in decades, centuries past, in terror and in war
have been erased from common thought

These briefly noted deaths
are lasting damning blows to kith and kin
to parents, siblings, lovers, children, friends
Their loss is not filled by tomorrow's further loss
Here is an accumulated grief
borne now and in all future time

I remember as I write
the spinster met in nineteen seventy-six
In her eighties and given passing help
fleeting attention from my time
not grudged but never repeated
She had a picture of her fiancé
in uniform for the First World War

Here was death in war
A love gone, a life alone

Hopes for laughter, children, Christmas, birthdays,
the falling out, the making up, the pleasures shared
all gone
Not in a news report
Not in a newspaper story
In a life altered

I heard the news today
When it is old
I hope I remember

James F Carnduff

Paint Pot

You would not think that a common pot of paint could exert so much anxiety in the user. Stop I am away ahead of myself, let me explain.

It all happened a week ago. I was redecorating the outside of a customer's villa and making a respectable job. I had finished for the day and as I walked home, taking a short cut over the downs, I stumbled over a tin which turned out to be a pot of paint. If I had only known then what I know now I would have left it alone. However curiosity got the better of me and I bent down and lifted it.

Looking closely at it I noticed that the writing on the side was in a foreign language. Never the less glancing around me I could not understand how a pot of paint should have come to be here. There was no road at this particular part of the Wiltshire downs, so I thought that I might as well have it, since paint of this calibre was expensive.

Sticking it in my haversack I trudged off home and forgot all about it. That is until Saturday when I was hanging my haversack in my work shed.

I wondered what colour the pot of paint was. I opened the tin and to my surprise the liquid was a sparkling gold.

What a gorgeous colour I thought. This would be perfect for my greenhouse which was badly needing a new coat of paint. Why don't I start now I could have it finished by supper time.

I then proceeded to dip my paint brush in the pot of paint and eagerly attacked the greenhouse.

To my surprise the paint flowed without effort over the wood of the greenhouse I did not even have to redip the brush in the paint pot.

I was about to have a rest when my wife called that lunch was ready so I left the paint brush across the lid of the paint pot and trooped off to have lunch.

After lunch I fell asleep and it was two hours later that I returned to the greenhouse to finish the painting. I was astonished to find that the paint had travelled out of the paint pot and had covered all the inside of the greenhouse including every pane of glass and was now proceeding to do likewise to the outside of the greenhouse.

I grabbed hold of the paint brush but unfortunately I got paint all over my hand and to my horror the gold paint was moving slowly over the skin of my hand and arm. It now seemed to have a mind of it's own as it methodically moved without stopping over my body.

I began to panic. How can I stop the wandering paint?

What kind of paint was this? I had never in my experience come across this predicament.

The gold paint was moving as if it had a purpose in mind and I was the purpose.

How do I stop this creeping gold paint? It was now moving up my neck and very soon it would be all over my face and hair. I would be smothered by the paint.

Horror upon horror.

Think! you fool I said to myself.

I must try to get the paint to stop or even better, back into the paint pot.

Lying on a shelf beside me was a 6 mm wood dowel, I grabbed it and put one end in my mouth and the other in the paint pot.

The paint was still moving over my face and had reached my mouth but instead of covering my face the paint moved down the wood dowel and emptied itself into the paint pot.

Saved by the bell! I thought.

The paint was now moving off my body into the pot and the greenhouse was being denuded of the gold paint as it finally all returned to the pot.

I breathed a sigh of relief. Grabbing the lid I replaced it firmly back on the tin as the last of the gold paint returned to the paint pot.

I put the paint pot carefully in my haversack and rushed off to return it to the path where I had found it.

As I was slowly returning home I met a man in a yellow oilskin which completely covered him. He asked me if I had seen a pot of paint.

I told him where he would find it and scurried off home.

About ten minutes later there was a very bright flash of light and what might have been a flying saucer zoomed overhead to disappear into the evening sky.

Wind

Who had whistled down the wind
As it effortlessly ripped away the storm jib
The sea frothed like Coca-Cola
Drowning us in chocolate sponge
The anchor said I'll hold
Trusty chain squealed I am old
Rusted weary
Then someone shut a storm door
While the yacht settled down
And reverberated the soulless night
A mill pond became it's surface
And galless gulls rested in silence
Far off in moon light façade
Spiders webs of a new camouflage
Revealing what is yet to come
God save all who sail the seas

By James F Carnduff

The Pebble

She drove. He sat in the passenger seat enjoying the scenery. They both had travelled this road before.

Loch lomond looked very tranquil and peaceful. He remembered that during the 1939/45 war he had hitchhiked carrying a 60lb. Rucksack, mainly because of rationing and had filled most of the room in his rucksack with tined food and anything which would not perish. Of course he expected to obtain a lift, as walking with this weight was not desirable.

The Scottish Youth Hostel Association had not long started so he did not require to carry tent and cooking utensils.

He was heading for Arrochar Youth Hostel, then over the hills to Crianlarich, on to Tyndrum and through Glencoe to the Ballachulish Bridge. It was here that he remembered the ferry, which carried 2 cars maximum load, and in the holiday season you sometimes had to wait 1 to 2 hours to cross. The alternate route was the long haul down the side of the loch through Kinlochleven and up the other side to North Balluchulish. What a difference the new bridge made now. They were soon negotiating the twisty road by the edge of loch Linnie and on towards Fort William.

They did not stop but carried on to pass Spean Bridge where the Commando Statue overlooks the glen along the side of Loch Lochy and cross by Loch Oich to Invergarry. As they headed west by the side of Loch Garry the afternoon sun sparkled on the still water. It was a picturesque scene.

"Why don't we stop here?" said John "It's quiet and pleasant!"

Joan stopped the car, parking it on a low mound which looked across the loch.

They unpacked their picnic basket and Primus stove and soon had the water for tea boiling merrily.

"What more could you ask for?" said John

"A good meal, a perfect cup of tea and a good cigar! It's unfortunate that I no longer inhale the wonder weed!"

"How far are you with your story called The Pebble?" asked Joan "You looked pensive as we were driving here?"

"Well" said John "I was thinking, looking at the landscape, how different the view would have been 2000 yrs ago with great swathes of deciduous and coniferous forests covering the landscape!"

207

"Is that how you start your story?" asked Joan.

"Yes and no! Here let me read you what I have produced so far!"

It was a time when the world was under nature's law. There was virtually no pollution, at least by man, the fact being that there were far fewer people than there is today.

Around 2000 years ago there lived in this pleasant land a king who ruled through knowledge and in a just manner.

It was at this time that his eldest son was born and the king named him Connor. The king loved his son greatly and on his twelfth birthday sent him to the abbey to receive his education, which would last for 5yrs. As well as reading and writing he would be coached in fencing, lance and horsemanship.

Connor returned on his 17th Birthday having completed his education. He excelled in all the fields he tackled. His father threw a great celebration of feasting and games in which his son showed his prowess.

On the third day of the celebrations, the king, to show his pride and love for his son, presented him with an white stallion, the fastest in the land.

Connor was delighted with his gift and thanking his father persuaded him to let him ride the stallion.

"Only if you take with you a company of armed men for protection?"

Connor willingly agreed signalling to a few of his friends to saddle up.

"If you are all ready we' ll race to the ford where the two rivers join. Whoever is last provides refreshments when we return."

Off he rode at great speed followed by the company of courtiers stretching out behind.

It was obvious that his stallion was the faster and he soon left them far behind. Connor soon reached the ford in record time and stepped down from his stallion and was about to drink the cool water, when from the other bank a vicious cry rang out followed by four bandits racing across the ford. Connor drew his sword and his long dagger and prepared himself as the first of the bandits rushed him. There ensued a melee of fighting but Connor skill disabled three of the bandits within minutes and he was fighting for his life with the forth bandit when he heard further yells as more of the bandits came racing across the river.

Just as Connor was preparing to fight the remaining bandits six of his companions arrived. Dismounting from their horses, even before they had come to rest, were soon in the battle chasing the defeated group of would be bandits back across the river.

"Are you alright, m' lord !"Exclaimed one of his companions.

"Yes!" retorted Connor "It was some fight, I am glad my sword skills were properly honed!"

As Connor said this he did not notice one of the bandits across the river bend down and remove a pebble from the bank and place it in his sling. Swinging it above his head he let fly with great force.

"Look out, m' lord!" Connor turned to look in the direction his companion had indicated but he was too late to escape the flying missile. It struck him on the side of his face at his temple. He gave a sigh and crumpled to the earth.

The bandit turned and laughed as he scampered off into the dense undergrowth.

***

The captain of the guard arrived and knelt beside the Prince.

"Is he dead?" he exclaimed.

"I don't think so, his breathing is very shallow!" said the companion.

"Right! you on horseback to the castle and explain what has happened, remember the Prince is still alive."

Off rode the messenger like the wind to prepare for the arrival of the wounded Prince.

"You two make a stretcher to sling between the horses to convey the Prince to the castle."

"Shall I take half a dozen men and chase after the bandits?"

"No!" replied the captain. "Our first priority is to return to the castle with the Prince, there will be time enough for that after we are back at the castle, gather up the Prince's sword and bring his horse."

Very soon the company were off to return to the castle. All too soon they arrived and were greeted at the castle gate by the King.

"Is he alive?" the King croaked. "Yes your majesty, but the druid healers should look after him."

"Yes, yes of course." groaned the King with tears in his eyes "Call the healers and take the Prince to his rooms, hurry!"

Eventually the druid healers arrived and ministered to the wounded Prince. The King was asked to wait outside while the healers gave orders for hot water, towels and special instruments to be brought to them, while they prepared to examine the Prince's wound.

To the King it seemed to take forever before the healers finally called him.

"How is my son?" demanded the King "Will he get well?" The healers just looked at the King and waited until his rush of words finally stopped.

"Please sit down your majesty and we will explain?" The King finally did as he was told seating himself in his armchair.

"Well " He demanded. "Speak?"

"As I am sure you realise," said the senior Druid Healer. "We have examined very carefully the wound the prince has received. A very small pebble striking his temple area on his right side caused it. The force with which the pebble struck was exceptional and has lodged just below the surface and extremely close to a main blood vessel in fact it has penetrated the blood vessel. It is because of the position of the pebble that we dare not remove it or dislodge it as this would cause a brain haemorrhage and bring about death."

"This is very serious." said the King "Is there nothing we can do to help the situation?"

"Yes!" said the senior druid "We have closed the wound in order that new skin will cover the wound. This is not a cure but if we keep him sedated for a short time and he is not allowed up to walk about for perhaps a month, he may recover his strength, but we must warn you that under no account can he risk, fencing, riding or anything boisterous for the rest of his life, as this could dislodge the pebble causing death. I am very sorry your majesty but there is nothing more can be done. We will however, be constantly at his side to replace his dressing and we will see that he understands fully his predicament."

Having given their verdict, two of the healers left while the third busied himself with the Prince's comfort.

As the weeks passed the King seemed to lose his joyous approach to life and began to show his age.

Connor, with the druid healers help managed to return to a semi- active roll. He decided, since he had to be immobilised, to spend his time in study. Before long the castle became a hive of scientific study with wise men from all over the world visiting the Prince to discuss many of the world's unsolved problems.

About this time the King suggested to Connor he should design and build a round tower house high above the castle where he could look out on all sides and see more of the kingdom.

Connor agreed and set to work designing and building his tower. However, many years had passed and the King died before the Prince's tower was finished and the crown now passed to Connor who became a wise King.

At last the tower was complete with its magnificent panoramic view from all sides. Connor spent a great deal of his time there and installed many of his most treasured books and manuscripts.

Time passed and he almost forgot about the pebble lodged in his temple but the occasional twinge reminded him to slow down and rest.

One day while he and his companions were discussing a problem regarding the kingdom, from the east a darkness approached the castle shutting out the day light.

"It's only twelve noon !" said the King. "Why is it so dark?" No one could answer why!

"Send for my wise men they may be able to shed some light on the matter?"

Very quickly the tower filled with all the wise and intelligent people in the castle. But no one could explain why this was happening. Some said "Ti's the end of the world!" others "That the gods were angry !"

"Is there no one who can answer my question?" asked the King in dismay. A servant approached the King and informed him that a strange monk was at the door requesting food and shelter. The King was about to dismiss the servant but thought and said "Bring this stranger here to me in the tower!"

The servant returned with the stranger monk and presented him to the King who looked him up and down.

"Do you wish food and lodging here?"

"If I may " replied the stranger

"Granted" said the King and paused "Can you tell me what and why this darkness has arrived?"

The stranger thought for a while and replied.

"I might, since I have learned many visions and abilities."

"Is there anything you need to help?"

"Yes I need a chair and I must face the east as that is the direction from which the darkness is approaching. One other thing, while I am seeing remember I am not in control and I am not responsible for what I see."

The King replied "I understand, nothing will happen to you no matter what you see, please begin."

The stranger sat down in the chair, resting his hands on the armrests, closing his eyes his head fell forward and for some time nothing happened, then his head lifted and with his eyes staring forward he began to speak.

"I see a land far far away. It is in turmoil. A great crowd has gathered to see prisoners being executed but this is no ordinary execution. Two of the prisoners, one is a thief the other a murderer but the one in the middle is a religious man in fact a holy man and has done no wrong. They are being crucified.

The murderer says "Why don't you take your self down from this cross that is if you are the son of god?"

The thief interrupts saying "This man is the Son of God!" and to the holy man

"Remember me?"

The holy man says "Today you shall be with me in Paradise. "and having said that he declared "Why have you forsaken me!" He then gave up his spirit to God.

The stranger opened his eyes saying

"Do you understand?"

"Yes!" extolled the King rising to his feet he drew his sword and with passion shouted "I will avenge this holy man!" As he said this the pebble in his brain was dislodged and he began to collapse but as he did so his sword fell from his hand in an arc burying the point in the wooden floor. At the very same moment, a shaft of light, came from the east to shine on the sword, causing it to glow with a golden light and at the same time transferring a dark shadow of the sword hilt on to the opposite wall revealing a Black Cross with a golden brightness surrounding it.

212

Ian Hunter

The Circle

Sho Loa Ling looked across the sea at the dying sun, its fire quenched on the distant horizon, boiling the ocean, making it pure. She raised her head high, higher, and gazed at the night, descending like a hood delicately pulled over this part of the world. She shivered. *He* had risen, she could feel it.

A few stars adorned the darkening sky, and there was the moon, its face marred, unlike her own pale, round face. Whatever troubled her was well hidden. It had to be.

She looked down, past the ramshackle homes, not so far different from the shacks which clinged tenaciously to the hills overlooking the rice fields in her distant land, then her gaze turned to the lights of the little taverna. She could hear music, a bouzouki playing, fast, joyful. Hands were being clapped, glasses struck against the scarred, battered tables in time to the music. Beyond that, something splashed through the water, coming towards them.

"They come."

Behind her, there was a long, weary sigh. "How many times have I told you not to talk !" snapped Jamie Connor. "You forget your place."

"I was merely –"

The tall Irishman strode across the room and towered above her. His arm moved back and she flinched instinctively, but he did not hit her, for once. "I am the Senior Apprentice, you are...." He smiled, but it only made his handsome face cruel. "The Lower Apprentice." He laughed. "The Loa Apprentice."

"I only –"

His hand darted out, closing on her cheeks and squeezing. "You are nothing, remember that ? Nothing. Tonight I will receive the Master's gift and become one with the night. You would do well to remember that, Sho Loa Ling."

She swallowed, tears in her eyes, but she could still talk, despite the pressure on her face. "You are a fool," she hissed.

Fury sparked through Connor's dark eyes, but he opened his hand, pushing her backwards. "We'll see who the fool is when I am changed and the Master has left you alone in the dark. Listen well to the night noises, little pale one, because one

215

of them might be me coming for you." He gestured towards the door. "Now, go. Get ready, they are the last to arrive."

She held his eyes, thinking what a poor vampire he would make. Striking and arrogant, but far too emotional, so unlike the Master. The Irishman would do well to last a tenth of the Master's long span before his tainted half-life came to an end.

*****

"Damn girl," Connor hissed, but she had her uses, for him as well as the Master. They each had desires which needed to be satisfied. He watched her leave the room, then slipped forward to take her place at the window, staring down at the small boat being tied to the little dock. Two figures lumbered on to the rickety timbers and walked closer. He smiled, hearing every word they were saying.

"I need a drink."

"Better to keep a clear head, and our wits about us."

"You think ?"

"I know. We are late, and Belanger may be displeased. We should hurry. The church is up ahead."

"Church ?"

"Don't worry, it is long abandoned."

Connor smiled. He could see them clearer now as they emerged from the last of the little homes to the start of the path that led to the church. One small and thin, clutching something to his chest. This was the misfit German wanted by the authorities while the other one was taller, wider, a bag over his shoulder. A traveller, he reckoned, one who had seen a bit of the world since being forced to leave his native America for crimes committed during the Civil War. Both men had a fair bounty on their heads, as had all of the Master's guests. There was a small fortune in infamy gathered here tonight. In fact, they had paid a small fortune to be here, for the chance of immortality, and to fund the Master's itinerate lifestyle. But even that payment did not secure them entry, there was the small matter of the Gift.

"What a godforsaken place. Who lives here ?" asked the smaller man, turning round.

"Fishermen mostly, living off the sea. Or sponge divers, taking their hauls to the bigger islands to sell at the markets."

"And still this place has a church ?" the German marvelled. "With a vampire inside ?"

"Belanger the Trickster, as he is sometimes known, perhaps he tricked God into leaving."

"I've heard he can hold silver," the little man said. "So the fact that he lives in a church should come as no surprise."

"I suppose not," agreed the American. "Maybe, our vampire is not a vampire after all, but a ghost."

"Yes," hissed his companion. "Pale and thin, with red eyes. Devil's eyes. Hot coals that can burn into your soul."

"Red eyes are the sign of the devil," the larger man rasped and spat on the ground for luck and to ward off evil spirits."

"If this Belanger is not a devil, then he is a demon, an imp in human form with pale skin and white, white hair. I heard it turned white because he was scared to death. He died and came back but his hair stayed white, and his body became that of an albino."

"Then pray the same thing does not happen to us," said the bigger man, laughing.

The smaller man laughed as well, and above them, Connor joined in.

"Something amusing you, Jamie ?"

Connor whirled. The Master was standing in the doorway, newly risen, looking more fragile than normal. The bloodlust would be uncoiling inside him, clouding his thoughts. This was a dangerous time for anyone who got in his way.

"No, no," Connor said quickly. "I was listening to the last of them arriving."

Belanger seemed to brighten a little at the news. "They are all here? Good. Go down and greet them, but search them thoroughly."

The Irishman hesitated. "But they come here willingly, master, on your invitation."

"I haven't survived this long by not being careful." Belanger pointed out. "Do you understand ?"

"Yes."

Of course, all the doors had been deliberately locked by the pale hand which went ahead of him, holding the other set of keys. So the dammed Chinese girl had got to them first, but the door was left wide open, revealing the scene to any passing Greek peasant.

Connor rushed forward, closed the door and locked it, then leaned back against the wood and sighed. This part of the church had been stripped bare. The floor empty save for the chest they had brought with them. There was nothing religious here, except intricate stain glass windows, depicting scenes which meant nothing to him, and even less now as only darkness pressed against them, denying them life. Fortunately there were many candles positioned about the room. The Master liked candles. He could spend forever staring into their flickering depths.

Connor pulled out his knife.

"Your bag, sir."

The big man looked at him and smiled, making his pock-marked face look even uglier. "I could make you eat that thing before you thought of using it."

Connor flicked the knife. "No, matter. My Master is a cautious man."

"Dead man, you mean," came the reply, but the large American carefully opened his bag and took something out, wrapped in paper. Slowly he unfolded it and held out his hand. "My payment."

The Irishman glanced at the jewelled scorpion. He had seen its kind before. Beautifully crafted, the stinger on a little hinge which allowed it to move. "It will do." He turned to the smaller man. "And you ?"

The German's large, round head nodded several times as he held out a leather bundle.

Connor wagged the knife.

"No, you open it."

The man nodded again, and struggled with the string that held the leather tight, but eventually he loosened the knot and rolled open the leather to reveal a doll.

Connor frowned. The doll had a cracked face, and a small coloured stone for one eye. He couldn't believe it. What a paltry gift. The Master would not accept this, and Connor would have to slit the little man's throat, and that would leave only eleven instead of twelve, and –

"For me ?" said a voice from behind.

Connor managed to hold the sigh inside him, and glared as Sho Loa Ling looked up at him, the faintest smile on her porcelain face. He gritted his teeth, fighting back his anger, forcing it down inside him, but later, when the sun was up, and the Master was at rest, he would let that anger rise, and so much more. Then he grimaced, remembering. he was going to be one of the Twelve, changed forever, his time of rising would forever be in time with the Master.

Belanger moved past, looking small, thin, and very, very pale, as if there was no blood left at all within his veins. Eight other men entered the room behind him, most of them wanted across Europe, a few had even faked their deaths to avoid capture and certain execution.

"Oh, I do like this," said Belanger, taking the broken doll. "And in her bridal clothes too." He laughed and looked at the bearer of the gift. "I'll bet this has a story attached to it ?"

"Yes," said the German. "It was – "

"Later," hushed Belanger, holding a finger to the little man's lips.

"Is this a joke, Belanger ?" a deep Scottish voice asked. "Some sort of sick perversion ?"

The albino grinned. "Oh, I do like the sound of that." Connor did his best to suppress his own smile. This was the Marquis of Carmichael and he was clearly unhappy about something.

The Scotsman jabbed out an accusing finger. "Don't be impudent, Belanger. I am referring to this....fellow."

Belanger held up his hand, indicating the tall, muscular black man whose own grin revealed perfect white teeth. Like rows of white tombstones, Connor thought.

"You mean Pearl Diver?" said the albino.

The Marquis looked disgusted. "That is his name?"

"And his occupation, as well," Belanger revealed. "Pirates employ him to kiss the ocean bottom to bring up treasures they have missed, sometimes in the pockets or around the throats of those they have thrown overboard. This dark pearl has paid handsomely to be here tonight."

"But still -"

The albino shook his head. "Still, his name is a legend in these parts, while you are a mere nobody, just another foreigner with a strange accent and even stranger manners."

The Marquis' mouth dropped open.

Belanger walked into the centre of the room. His red eyes began to glow and change colour. One of the men muttered something, a prayer, perhaps. Connor smiled. God was long gone from this place.

"Every hundred years I bestow this gift," said Belanger. "Twelve form the circle, eleven mortal men, and me, but the eleven leave changed."

Connor looked round. Sho Loa Ling was moving to the chest in the corner, opening it and taking out something she cradled to her breast.

"My apprentice will give you your fangs, gentlemen. They are sharp, but hollow. You will suck blood and swallow it."

Connor held out his hand and accepted the fangs. The others had placed them into their mouths, grinning widely. They looked like imbeciles, but for all that, they were somehow unsettling, like mad, capering apes.

He watched Sho Loa Ling pad back to the chest and return with a bottle.

"Sho Loa will mark the spot on the throat where you must bite, and swallow fast, blood is too precious to waste."

Connor sniffed as she opened the little stopper and something sharp assaulted his nostrils. She walked among them, dabbing each one on the throat, staining it yellow.   All except him.

He turned, heart pounding.

"Never fear, Jamie," Belanger told him. "I know where to bite you."

He nodded. Of course, the Master was going to bite him. It was an honour.

Belanger, stepped back and clapped his hands. "Now gentlemen, form a circle, one behind the other. No, Pearl Diver, I think you should go behind the Marquis."

Pearl Diver grinned.

"Enough of this insolence," snarled the Scotsman. "No black will touch my skin, let alone bite it. You have had your fun, Belanger, but now I am leaving."

The pale vampire strode across the room and grabbed him by the hair. The nobleman turned and lashed out at the albino's chest. Roam ignored the blows and seized the arm and squeezed. "I don't need you, not really," he said calmly, as if his words were of no importance. "I could kill you now and go down to the taverna and get a Greek fisherman to take your place. Do you want that ?"

The Marquis spoke through gritted teeth. "No."

"Then stand in front of the Pearl Diver."

Nursing his arm, the nobleman reluctantly did as he was told.

Connor looked over his shoulder. Belanger was positioning the little man who had brought the doll behind him, making him stand on a small wooden crate. Connor took his position in front of his master.

"That's it, now move round everyone. Bend forward slightly, and drink," Belanger told them. "Drink and be transformed."

Belanger moved, fangs slipping into place, gasping slightly as the little man bit him in the neck, and he punctured Connor's skin, and the Irishman leaned forward, biting the man in front, and so it went on. A strange dance, an even stranger embrace. Not without difficulty, but it had been done before, and before that, so many times.

As it would be again.

He smiled, hearing them gasp and groan, hearing them gulp down the blood which gushed into their mouths.

And he fed too, Jamie Connor flowing into him, all of his petty little life, so different from the starving youth he had taken under his wing years ago. Innocent then, but now a monster, one he had created, and while this was distasteful, feeling these things, in a way, it was his duty. Connor had been his creation. Poor Sho Loa Ling. How she had suffered. He would have to make it up to her.

Now he could feel them all, as they filled up with each other's blood, choking on it, but never fast enough to replace their own diminishing supply. Memories echoed around inside his head. He was there at the bottom of the sea when a shark brushed past a youthful Pearl Diver, and he shared his panic and desire to race to the surface. He was here, right now, as the Marquis made a fortune from the slave trade, plucking people from Africa and killing most of them on the way to the new world. The little man behind him was there too, and Belanger sought out those memories in particular, and here was the story behind the doll and the little girl it had belonged to.

Ah, perfect.

In front of him, Connor was dying, they all were.

And Belanger continued to feed, as all the thoughts and memories and everything in the heads of the eleven men began to fade, replaced by panic, but death had them now, holding them tight.

"Enough !" he said, stepping back, letting go, and Connor fell away, glassy eyes looking at nothing.

One by one, they toppled over, except for the little man behind him. Belanger reached back and tried to push him off the wooden crate, but the little man clung on tenaciously to his neck in a strong, death grip. Roam gave up and reached back, fingers lengthening, becoming sharp and serrated, and he gripped the little man's face, and squeezed tighter, digging into skin and muscle. With a gasp he tore off the lower jaw, and grimaced as it took a junk of his neck with it. The little man crumpled on to the floor.

Roam sighed and suddenly laughed out loud at the sight of the ebony form of Pearl Diver lying across the Marquis of Carmichael, dark arm wrapped around the nobleman's body. They looked so peaceful, like lovers united forever in death.

Sho Loa Ling rushed forward, holding up his cloak. He wrapped it around his body and stared at the eleven dead men littered on the floor.

"All changed, monsters and monsters-to-be," he muttered, gazing at Connor's body, then looked at the slight Chinese girl in front of him. He reached out and brushed her cheek. "You are Senior Apprentice now, and we will find an assistant for you soon, I promise."

"Yes, Master," she said, bowing. "Thank you, Master."

"I have to go," he told her. "My mind is awash with thoughts and dreams. Memories and atrocities. I must commit them to paper. When I am finished, we will leave here. I will wait in the boat, while you burn this place. Candles can be such deceptive things, beautiful, but so dangerous if left unattended. Do you understand ?"

"Yes, Master."

He smiled. "But until then, I think you will find some hollow fangs in the chest that might fit a mouth as small as your own. Why don't you amuse yourself with Connor's body until I am ready ?"

Sho Loa Ling smiled.

Belanger nodded, watching her skip across the floor, leaving a trail of bloody footprints. Rather like my own across history, he thought, closing the door as she turned with a sharp mouth and bright, eager eyes.

Too Hot to Handle

You are a hot curry
Four chillies on the menu
Coming with a warning
From the waiter
Taken with two jugs
Of water
And leaving a metal
Flavour behind
Making everything that follows
Taste strange
Taste wrong

Jesus of Suburbia

I'll be there when they come for him
On the barricades
Because of him I never run out of beer
Or fish fingers
Now we charge when tours come round
Unless he's levitating
Then everyone can see him
But I try and spoil as many pictures
As I can
By putting my hand in front of
Their lenses
You want your pet brought back from
The dead, kid?
Then it's gonna cost you

Taking Back Sunday

It started slowly
Shops closed
Shopping centre car parks
were deserted
except for a few trolleys
snagging wind-tossed litter

Restaurants and pubs
followed
Boys who did paper
rounds stayed in bed

There was no news
no live radio
no live anything
Repeats filled the TV channels
before even they stopped
replaced by old test cards
or fuzzy blackness

Some people claimed
to have seen a giant ghost
hand descend on them
The tip of a phantom
index finger touch their forehead
and a booming voice
command
REST
then gentler, rest, rest
Pushing them towards bed
to awaken refreshed on
a Monday that didn't
seem so bad after all

Saturday is Martyn Bennett Day

And Celtic Connections are
hosting two commemorative events
But if you can't make it
take one of his albums
Grit, perhaps, that would do
Hold it in your hand
Edge running along your thumb and index finger
like a stone you are about to skim over water

Then attack the wall
Slicing through paint and paper,
plaster and brick
Don't stop
even when it hurts
When your skin starts to tear
muscle and bone and CD fuse together
and you break across the borderlands
to where death healed him
And you can hear the keening, calling pipes
full of the sound of loss and love,
joy and sorrow
and everything in between

My Happiness Is Past Its Sell-by Date

Happiness used to be just that
Then they did what they did
with Marathon Bars (now Snickers)
and Opal Fruits (now Starburst)

Happiness became Cheerfulness
Re-named
Re-branded
Re-packaged

Soon it disappeared from the shelves
only available from specialist shops
then not at all
as EC Directives were implemented
concerned about the effects
flavours, colours and additives
might have on
your mind
your heart
your soul

I kept a little bit of happiness
in the freezer
wrapped in cling film
but it was there too long
chipped out of shape
trying to get the polythene off
its flavour gone

Mary Strick

On an African Farm.

Like the famous film, my story starts, "I had a farm once, in Africa". It was in South Africa, in what was then the Transvaal Province.

If you had – as they do in such films - overflown on the Summer afternoon of my story, you would have spied a little blue pick-up bustling out of a farm gateway. Down the sandy road, past the barking bull terrier at the Francis's farm, past the entrance to the immediate neighbours it drove, slowing down at the sharp corner in case the loopy Smit son was roaring out of his gate without looking. In sparse traffic, people grow careless! With mother in law, who was visiting to inspect our new farm, I was bound for the Farmers' Co-Operative, a vast corrugated-iron wonderland of farming requirements both large and small. We were on an interior decorating mission.

As everybody did, Gran had smiled when she first saw the house, shaped like an upended matchbox. "Well, it's different," she said. Of the two steps between scullery and kitchen, "These will be a nuisance." And, approvingly, "I'm glad there's a downstairs bedroom." But when she walked into the long, narrow, disproportionately tall lounge, words failed her.

Three ugly stone pillars supported an upstairs walkway, their stone undressed to the point of nakedness, as was an indoor flower box. This, Mrs. Pete Pumpkin had proudly assured us, "goes right down into the outside soil". She hadn't added that if you rounded it carelessly you would be sure to damage an ankle on its naked stonework.

And then there were the windows, floor to high unceilinged roof, installed by Pete Pumpkin, previous farmer and "architect". Come from a demolished luxury city hotel, they were a job-lot he'd got from a friend "in salvage". He had fancied a louvre effect and had mounted, in three blocks, eight very large rectangular windows per block, one on top of the other, but sideways, to open outwards. But did they help to cool the lounge? This was a west-facing room so rising air caught in those huge outwardly projecting panes must surely be very hot.

After a while, with unwonted tact, Ma spoke. "You should hang curtains in the lounge, Mary. In winter, you'll need to close out the dark and the draughts".

I made no response.

She added, "And they would camouflage the windows".

"But the cost," I wailed, "we can't afford to buy enough material to curtain those huge windows".

I should have known that my resourceful mother-in-law, who achieved wonders of improvisation as a matter of course, would find an answer. "We'll get some hessian".

And so the little blue van was taking us to the Co-Op, where we bought a whole bolt of hessian. A "boy" was detailed to load it while we walked next door to the General Dealer's store and were lucky to find fabric dye in stock. "But this'll be too bright," I whinged, "it's Pillar Box Red!" "Nonsense," retorted Gran, "it'll be toned down by the hessian and be just fine. You'll see". Back home, while daylight lasted (for as yet the settlement had no electricity) we cut the hessian into six suitable lengths, and collected a great mound of firewood.

Next day we made a big fire in the shade of a row of Pepper trees, trusting that since they were both hardy and very green they wouldn't catch alight. We borrowed a trivet from the cook-girl, and set on it a huge cast-iron black pot, a "kaffir pot" in those politically incorrect days. (From its original meaning of indigenous inhabitant this word has become an ultimately insulting one.) Looking as though cannibals were busy, the red dye came to the boil and bubbled throatily. We fed in the hessian two lengths at a time, pushed it under with sticks, then vigorously stirred the evil-looking stew.

Under the combined onslaught of afternoon heat and roaring fire, our faces were soon flushed and shiny, our hair lank. We circled watchfully, adding fuel to our fire, prodding our cauldron and shrieking with near hysterical laughter. MacBeth's witches would have welcomed us to the Sisterhood.

After more or less the correct amount of time had elapsed to set the dye, we carefully used our long sticks to remove the hessian. To avoid being burnt by the splashing brew or the hot sacking, fast reflexes were needed to time the necessary sideways jumps. Eventually we were done and tipped the pot over to empty it. I hope the Buddhists are wrong about plants having feelings, else that grass must have been screaming in pain.

The fabric turned out a vibrant but pleasant rust shade which, we felt, disguised the hessian origins. We left our cheerful curtains-to-be spread out to dry overnight. Once they had cooled off a little we patted them as flat as we could on the lumpy grass where twigs and little grape-like bunches of pink pepper seeds lay everywhere. Without electricity I wasn't proposing to use a flat iron to smooth them!

The next task was to sew on tapes and insert hooks. No hems; we reasoned that if they frayed it would look like artistic fringing. Assisted by one of our "boys" (in the Old South Africa, no matter his actual age, a Black worker was always a "boy") we battled to hang the long, heavy curtains. The great height caused antics befitting trapeze artists or monkeys. Two of the windows were relatively easy as they had a halfway-house cement ledge to stand on, but one was just a wall of windows, frame mounted on frame. Stepping out from the first floor landing, I stood on an opened window frame, clutched one-handedly to a higher one, and with the other worked the burdened curtain rod into position on its brackets. I don't suffer from vertigo.

All done and hung, we admired our handiwork, well satisfied with results. We felt it looked positively House and Garden. Moses (the 50-something "boy") grunted with satisfaction and pronounced the result, "Good... Ja, goed".

But then our youngest came in from play and delivered the punch-line. "Mummy, why have we got sacks hanging in our windows?" he asked.

Printed in the United Kingdom
by Lightning Source UK Ltd.
121641UK00003B/58-84/A